The
Water Thief

Nicholas Lamar Soutter

Thanks:

Customarily acknowledgements are brief.

But since I'm reasonably sure that the only people who ever read them are those mentioned in there anyway, I feel no obligation to shorten anything on anyone's behalf.

First I'd like to thank my wife. If she had any brains at all—I mean ANY (and keep in mind, she'll be reading this)— she'd have headed for the hills when I told her I was a writer. Let's face it, little girls need dental care, fairy-princess costumes, and round the clock GPS tracking. Whether through my charm (who are we kidding?), or money (nope) or by trickery (well…), she has stayed with me and supported my career.

Now, when I started writing, I did what all rookie novelists do; I surrounded myself with inferior writers. It gives you a boost, makes you feel good about your own skills. But it's a terrible waste of time. You need to spend time with authors who are better than you are. It hurts, but it's the only way to get good. To that end, I'd like to thank Philomena for wasting her time with me.

I'd like to thank my sister, Liz. Her determination and skill is an inspiration in my own life and work.

I'd also like to thank my father and stepmother who, over my explicit objections, forced me to get an education.

My aunt Emily… I've been through some rough times, and I'm not sure that there's anybody who's been there for me more—everybody should be so lucky.

My Aunt Diane… your friendship means more to me than you know.

Kathy, Nichole, and Liz, thank you. Without your meticulous line edits people might realize that I can't write.

To Nyira: your support in all my work has always meant more than you know.

Pat, Harvey, thank you both.

Last, but not least, thank you to John Paine, Scarlett Rugers, and Joe Correa.

Wow, so many more I'd like to thank… I'm sure I neglected a number of people. If you're at all offended that I forgot you, please chalk it up to obscenely high doses of Oxycontin.

For My Wife Holly, and for
Emily and Alyssa

"Capitalism is the astounding belief that the most wickedest of men will do the most wickedest of things for the greatest good of everyone."

−John Maynard Keynes

"Capitalism is not about free competitive choices among people who are reasonably equal in their buying and selling of economic power. It is about concentrating capital, concentrating economic power in very few hands, using that power to trash everyone who gets in their way."

−David Korten

1

First there would be poker, then the executions. It's perverse to dwell on the suffering of others, but on the first Monday of every month I couldn't think about much else. On the days I bathed, I'd hold the soap in my hands and wonder if it was rendered from the fat of someone I had seen strung up, maybe even someone I knew. Did it come from their stomach fat? From someone's dimpled thighs? I think probably the fat from all the people executed publicly was melted together with everyone else reclamated that day, or sold at mark-up for the novelty of it.

I also wondered if it bothered anybody else, this monthly spectacle. There was no way to tell, of course. Everybody watched together on television, whooped and hollered in delight with each drop, placed bets on whether the neck would break, or on how long it would take the writhing to stop. Just like I did.

Beatrice took the car that morning, so as usual I was on my bike. It was a god-awful contraption—I had to work to keep the pedals from sliding off the crank arm, the handlebars were loose, the struts were rusted out, and it had no brakes to speak of. At any moment the clunker could send me careening into oncoming traffic. My right leg, which always hurt in bad weather, was now seizing up on me. Still, all I could think about were the hangings.

Maybe that was why I had an anxiety disorder.

I hadn't brought my pills with me. If I had, I'd have been tempted to use them. Linus disapproved, and he could always tell. I decided on a cigarette instead, but I had to be quick about it. My permit was for outdoor smoking only, and the sky was getting darker, the wind had picked up, and the sulfur in the air was getting stronger. I put the executions out of my mind and pedaled to work as fast as I could.

I was a private citizen, which is to say that I was the private property of the Ackerman Brothers Securities & Investments firm. They held most of my futures, which meant that even though I worked for them, they took back much of my income as dividends. That was why my smoking permit had cost so much. Some poor actuary had to sit down and calculate it all out—my future earnings potential and what effect my smoking might have on it, the sympathetic effects on colleagues, collateral damages to third parties and the environment, and so on. It took them nine months to calculate the base line and they had to re-figure it every quarter to account for changes in the market. It was a nightmare of accounting.

Sometimes I think that's the reason I took up smoking— my own little rebellion against the system. If everybody lit up, maybe we could choke the firm on its own paperwork.

I rode up to work, one of the thousands of anonymous Ackerman administrative buildings that dotted the region. It was an old red brick-and-mortar monstrosity. The bricks were cracked and covered in dirt, rust, and sclerotic fungus. I wheeled past a large field in front with tall air-horn speakers posted at the corners. Morning calisthenics had already started, and the tinny voice of our CEO, Takahiro Takashi, boomed out over the yard.

I locked up my bike, pulling my satchel from the back. The tan canvas bag was bursting with the loose-leaf papers, pamphlets, and clippings I had collected earlier that morning. With the bag slung over my shoulder, I slipped behind the building.

I pulled out my tobacco and worked quickly, using the corner for cover. I leaned my shoulder into the wall, shielding the loose leaves as I rolled the cigarette tight and licked it closed.

"Colleague?"

A young man in dark blue police overalls appeared behind me, an AK-47 slung over his shoulder. I had seen him before, trolling the yard for infractions he could levy.

"Do you have a license for that?" he asked.

The guy was a noob, fresh and stupid on an order of magnitude I hadn't seen in a good long time. Sure, a cop *could* go around catching criminals, but there was no real money in it. Good cops (the rich ones anyway) knew it was a lot easier to make their criminals. If my permit wasn't in order, his commission would be a lot higher if he waited till I lit the thing to bust me. Heck, a really good cop would have found a way to get me to offer him one.

Of course, making criminals wasn't perfectly safe, either. Another cop could catch you doing it, or you could hassle the wrong guy at the wrong time and find yourself on the business end of a fine so big you'd be facing the rendering vats. The right amount of attitude with the cops went a long way towards convincing them that you were that guy, and this was that time.

I pulled out my ledger, that small, ubiquitous electronic tablet which contained the sum of my total financial life— from the in-utero debts I had incurred suckling nutrients from my mother, to how much I paid in estimated air charges last year.

"Your name Charles Thatcher?"

I nodded.

I was reasonably sure my permit was in order. Still, there were a million different ways they could get you if they wanted. There were an infinite number of contracts, clauses, exceptions, amendments and corrections which, in spite of the loud and oft repeated assurances from the best legal minds at Ackerman, I was reasonably sure nobody fully understood. That was the beauty of the system—everybody was so busy interpreting and litigating the little details of everyday life that nobody could organize for any other purpose. Rebellion, insurgency, revolution, all of these were impossible; civil unrest litigated out of existence.

I even had insurance against nuisance challenges to my permit, for just that reason. This guy probably went around hitting people with tiny violations that were cheaper to pay off than to fight in court. Idiots always dragged down the efficiency of a market.

He held my ledger and thumb-swiped through the details of my permit, grimacing as he read. He tried to salvage a few caps off me by asking why I wasn't in the yard for calisthenics, but we both knew it wasn't going anywhere.

"Medical waiver," I said.

It was a lie. My right leg had been crushed years ago, and while I still had the scars, it rarely gave me much trouble. But let's face it, calisthenics sucked. I exaggerated a recent flare-up to a doctor who wasn't being paid quite enough to do a thorough exam, and was willing to take a few extra caps to attest to things that weren't strictly speaking true. Lo and behold, no jumping jacks for six months. And I have to say, though the exercises are mandatory, I'd never seen the C-Level executives (like the CEO, CBO, or CAO) doing them—except for special events. Our Chief Financial Officer was pushing three hundred and fifty pounds. But he was the CFO, so I assume he could afford a better waiver than I could.

The rain started in earnest now. The cop glared at me before handing me my ledger and walking away. In the meantime my cigarette had dissolved into mush in my hand. Careful not to give him an excuse by littering, I shoved the goop into my overalls and went inside.

2

The lights in the lobby were off, and I could see only by the dim glow of the overcast skylight. Simon sat behind the security desk and, as my eyes adjusted, it looked to me like he was reading a book.

"Aren't you going to turn on the lights?" I asked.

"Still early," he said, solemnly.

I looked at my watch, but I couldn't make out the time. I lifted my hand and, sure enough, I couldn't even count the fingers just six inches from my face.

Who is he kidding with that book? There's no way he could be reading it.

I waited to see if he'd turn a page. Nothing. I could hear my own clothes rustling as I walked to the bench at the far side, where I unzipped my overalls, climbed out and straightened myself up, letting my suit and tie breathe.

"They have lockers, you know," said a gloomy voice.

I sighed, pulled out a single cap and placed it on the desk. "Yeah, but there's a new insurance surcharge. I haven't had time to file for it, and without it someone's going to swipe my stuff."

Simon just kept reading. He didn't even glance towards the cap. He might have been holding out for a five instead, but in that light I could have put a twenty under his nose and he wouldn't have known it.

Shouldn't he have turned the page by now?

"Looks like rain," I announced as I packed my overalls.

"It's always raining."

"Not always," I said, trying to be cheery. "Besides, rain is a good thing. It takes the sulfur out of the air. If we go too long without it, the next big storm eats through the roof of your car."

"Turns my hair green," he said, twisting the fragile, sickly colored strands with his finger.

"Well, you wouldn't be the first. Get an umbrella," I said. "Weathador makes a great one, cheap too."

"Sucks to an umbrella," he replied. "It'll last a few months then I'll have to replace it. They can't make me buy one."

It's the executions, I thought excitedly. But I had known Simon almost a year, and if the executions bothered him, this was the first he'd ever shown it. Besides, anybody who was so obvious in his dislike of anything Ackerman did was going to get picked off quick.

"Nobody's making you buy one. I just thought—"

"Of course they're making me buy it," he said, putting the book down. "That's what they do."

"Who?"

He didn't answer. I wondered if it was too late to go out into the field and do my push-ups.

The cap remained on the desk, unmolested. I had the distinct impression that he was watching me. I couldn't see his face, but I was sure that somehow he could see mine. I nodded to him and headed for the stairs as quickly as I could.

"They're out," Simon interjected, returning to his book.

"The stairs are out?" I asked. "They're stairs, how can they be 'out'?"

"Maintenance. They're replacing the banister. You'll have to take the elevator."

The elevator would take a load off my leg, but at five cents a floor, that would be thirty-five up and thirty-five down. Do that twice a day, plus lunch, that's a cap forty for the day. Not a lot, but a couple hundred employees came in and out of the seventh floor alone, and the building had twelve floors. Yep, they'd rake in a little dough.

Well, at least it's not government.

The seventh floor was where all the mid-grade Perception Management colleagues worked. We had no windows or offices, just four corners and rows upon rows of cubicles. The only fixed lights were tracks of tiny bulbs that ran along the floors, like on an airplane. They gave off just enough of a glow to make out the corridors winding through the constantly shifting maze of charcoal gray partitions.

I offset the cost of my cubicle by sharing it with a colleague named Bernard Milton. Bernard was a short man, stocky—well, let's be honest—fat really (bursting out of his suspenders fat). He had thin, sparse hair, which had prematurely developed mousy gray strands, and he was always eating chocolates, caramel candies or cookies, which left his face, hands and scalp with a permanent greasy sheen. Living in the shadows of the seventh floor, you could never be sure he wasn't eavesdropping on you from behind some partition, or in a dark corner waiting to swipe something from your desk. An Alpha once called him (with both a little affection and a good deal of malice) "Gollum"—a wretched creature from an ancient fiction. The name stuck.

I pretended not to hear it, or that I was above using it, but Bernard *was* a wretched colleague. He hardly ever worked. He just spent his time rummaging the building for anything of value. Spot him skulking away, and you could bet something was missing from your desk. He even took the cheap things, like paperclips, binders, and pushpins. A few years ago some colleagues took to setting up infrared taser traps in their cubicles. But soon the traps began disappearing. Before long all the suppliers were out of stock, except for Bernard, who was selling off a surplus.

His one redeeming feature was that he was horrible at poker. He's the only man I've ever met who was irrefutably worse than I was. Poker was so ubiquitous, such a symbol of affluence and influence, that it was nice not to be the worst player on the floor. His set was second hand—two torn cardboard leather shooters and six worn and mismatched dice. I mean he could play the game, shoot the dice, and keep them hidden. But he was easy as all hell to read. If he just had a bunch of random numbers, he'd be sweating bullets. If he threw a few pairs or triplets (especially high ones), he'd be wriggling with glee. If that poor guy ever rolled six sixes he'd probably die of a heart attack. That was the only reason he hadn't found his morning coffee laced with strychnine; anybody truly upset with his antics could usually win enough off him to let it go.

My desk had the usual stack of thirty or so memos that had collected overnight. Ackerman did everything on real paper—watermarked and numbered—to slow the rate of corporate espionage. The memos were all the usual bureaucratic nonsense: Action Item Change Requests now needed to be signed by hand, the tariff for failing to write legibly in the "pertaining" field of incident reports had been increased four cents, sixth-floor colleagues were no longer to use the seventh-floor vending machines unless their grade was Delta or better....

I was happy to get a jump on the day, what with everyone else still out in the yard. I put on my glasses (my father's old wire-framed ones), turned on the green-screen terminal, and began checking the stocks and futures markets so I could ration out my resources for the week. With paper and a pencil, I noted any troubling changes in the market. The cost of electricity had gone up. I eyed my small desk lamp, wondering if I could lower the wattage any more. Paper prices were steady, and so was the cost of air. The price of coffee had plummeted—good news that would save me some money when I had lunch with Linus.

But when I saw the price of water I nearly choked. In the last hour it had gone up tenfold. Buying some more information, I learned that there had been an attack, this time at a water treatment facility in Brookhurst. A corporation from a competing Karitzu paid a mercenary firm to blow it up, and raw sewage was now spilling into the aquifer.

My God! Did this happen before my shower? What about the toilet? Christ, I may have just blown six hundred caps on a single flush!

Hell, for the next few hours I couldn't even afford to wash my hands.

My ledger beeped. I pulled it out and checked the screen. It was the MWS (Market Warning Service), an insurance firm who had sold me a warning package to notify me of wild shifts in the market.

They wanted to tell me that the price of water was going up.

My face became flushed. I clenched my fists and resisted the urge to lash out. I cursed the bombers—terrorists and looters with no sense of decency. I cursed MWS, which seemed to notify me of these swings much later than their higher-paying customers. Then I laid into my insurer, the Market Instability Insurance Company, who, if I actually filed a claim, would drown me in a tidal wave of paperwork or just cancel my policy on a technical issue.

But I wasn't upset at any of these things. Not really.

I was upset that no matter what I did, no matter how hard I researched it, I would never know the real reason that water prices had jumped.

Sure, the story claimed that there had been a bombing. But it was just as likely an industrial accident managed to look like an attack. Or maybe the incident was staged to give Ackerman an excuse to raise prices. Heck, maybe a group of executives had gone long on water stocks and engineered the blast to corner the market. I could put a million caps into researching it, and I'd still never know for sure.

Oh, I'd have been a rich man if in that moment I could have sold my hatred.

But there was no time for ruminating. Soon every colleague I knew would be breathing down my neck. So I finished checking the markets and went to work.

It began getting brighter on the seventh floor as colleagues started coming in; the reassuring sound of keyboards, typewriters, and idle chatter all waking up for the day. No one would be talking about the water; why should they—you could short sell the stock and make a killing until it became common knowledge. A lot of money was going to be changing hands.

I closed the curtains to protect what little light I had—moochers were always trying to sneak some reading light when you weren't looking. I picked up my satchel, pulled out the literature and fanned it across the desk. I was a Delta-grade colleague from Perception Management. Delta was my contract grade, and Perception Management was the division of Ackerman that dealt with unfavorable press, ratings, or reviews. In the mornings I would pick up whatever literature I could, then spend the day scouring it and writing reports, which I would send to the ninth floor for further review. I earned a commission on any report that made or saved the firm money.

The first and most obvious incident was an article in the *Scientific Review Daily*, which had said that they had found fillers, like sawdust and powdered plastics, in a number of Ackerman-branded baby formulas. This might seem like an obvious write-up, but it was a lead story, and by now there were probably hundreds or even thousands of Ackerman colleagues reporting it. The only people who would make a dime from it were the early reporters, people who paid off the local newspapers to get the story before it was off the press. By now it was worth fractions of a penny.

You couldn't look for stories like this, things that stood out. The art to finding a quality incident was in looking for what was discreet. Run away from anything bold, underlined, highlighted, glowing, or in those metallic inks that change color. Literature was designed to be eye catching, to draw attention. The professional perception manager was drawn to the things people ignored.

The first good incident I found was an article on a youth soccer league that couldn't practice because their last ball ruptured on a hard kick. It looked like a sad story, until you realized that they needlessly mentioned the brand of the ball (an Ackerman subsidiary). This wasn't an account of some poor soccer team; it was a takedown piece about Ackerman dashing the hopes and dreams of a bunch of kids. I clipped the story and wrote up a report. I suggested that we argue that they had over-inflated the ball, hit them with a modest fine for slander, and warn them (for their own sake) about making libel claims in the future without first having an expert determine the actual cause of failure. Then we mention that Ackerman-branded soccer balls actually have failure rates far below average (which they might) and direct people to the nearest retailer. I took all of these suggestions, put them into the pneumo tube and sent them off for review.

Next I found a wonderful story on how one of Ackerman's diet pills was causing dangerously low levels of calcium in the blood. Some people were even getting rickets. I recommended a few ways to discredit the findings. I also forwarded a copy of my report to Marketing. That way, if there was any truth to the story, they could rebrand the pills as a cure for calcium-induced arthritis.

While my approach was to find the subtle stories, it wasn't the only way to eke out a living on the seventh floor. The Shotgun was a common strategy too: submit as many reports as you can, as fast as possible, in the hopes that you hit something. The Poachers were people who never paid for literature, but spent all their time trying to gleam stories from "casual" chats with colleagues. Leoben, one of the managers, was a quintessential Stabber—working just enough to look busy, all the while making his principal income from ratting out colleagues for crimes, real or imagined, against the firm.

Bernard, on the rare occasions he actually worked, was a Nuker. He would find the most obscure article, a ludicrous or innocuous account about nothing in particular, which drew nobody's interest. He'd spend hours researching and writing up long, fantastical yarns on how, if the planets aligned just right and the rules of gravity shifted for a moment, as a parallel universe opened up and suspended the laws of physics as we know it, this article might just represent the worst thing *ever* to happen to Ackerman Brothers (if not the universe as a whole). He'd highlight it, put little arrow stickers all over it, tie it in a ribbon, stick it in the pneumo tube, and send his dire predictions on their merry way.

A supervisor called Bernard's work genius.

Thane Corbett, on the other hand, had his hands in many different pies. He wrote only a few reports a day. He worked hard on them and did a professional, solid job (though they were never quite the masterpieces he thought they were). The rest of the time he was working on so many different things that it was impossible to remember just which was his current get-rich-quick scheme. He'd invested in a traveling carnival for a while, then in professional mentoring. He was taking a course in sub-zero wilderness survival, presumably to lead expeditions into the wasteland outside Capital City. His latest serious project was real estate, buying up Low Security (LowSec) neighborhoods and squeezing them for every penny he could.

I finished a number of other stories that morning. One was a particularly alarmist Op-Ed on how Perception Management, as a practice, was leading to artificially inflated stock prices that would result in a global economic collapse. Another defamatory story claimed that Ackerman had assassinated an executive from a rival corp. Lastly, there was an article that argued that our influence within the Karitzu had grown too strong.

I packed my things, ready to head out for my lunch with Linus Cabal. As I headed out through the curtains, I caught an elbow straight to my face. I stumbled back and then toppled to the ground. My literature flew into the air and scattered across the room—Bernard's own papers tossed into the mix.

"Oh my god," Bernard said, "I... I... I didn't see you. Oh, I hope you're not hurt?" He made a mad dash for the clutter of papers. He scrambled over them, but his fingers were so thick that he couldn't slide his thumb under them, so he hastily stuffed crumpled fistfuls of literature into the crook of his arm.

"Get out!"

"Just let me get my papers, a million apologies!" he said.

"Those aren't yours!"

"Oh, well they're all pretty much the same among colleagues, eh? We're all on the same team. I'm sure I saw a few land on your desk. Let me see... Say, have you seen Corbett? I was hoping to get a ride home. Ever since I got mugged, well, I just don't..." he stuttered.

"Get out!" I cried, shoving the oaf out of our cubicle. He vanished in the darkness, a trail of crumpled papers behind him. The damage was done; anything of any value was gone, and what was left behind was mostly the junk he had brought in with him.

For a moment I considered what the firm would charge me if I put a bullet between his eyes. It would have to cover all his futures—probably not enough that they'd hang me for it, but they might hock a few of my organs. Maybe I could find a way to convince Linus to cover the tab. He certainly wouldn't care if I killed anyone. But Linus didn't do favors—he collected debts, and a debt to him was never fully repaid.

No, it was fun to joke about, but the math was against me.

Frustrated, I began straightening up the mess. I didn't have the budget to buy more literature, so I'd have to try to salvage something from the scraps he'd left.

As I was tossing the stray papers into my safe, a page caught my eye. It was simple, delicate, an Ackerman court record—printed on a piece of tissue paper so thin that it was translucent—almost impossible to scan or copy. *Why would anyone bother with a court record? They're expensive, and trials are for litigators, not Perception.*

"Memo," cried an Epsilon, blindly thrusting a sheet into the cubicle. I took it, tossed it into the trash and went back to the report.

The story covered the arrest and preliminary hearing of an Epsilon, a terribly low-ranked woman named Sarah Aisling. She had been living in LowSec, the last bastion of anything that resembled civilization before the destitute wasteland outside, and home to a vast number of poor, low and null-contract colleagues and employees from smaller corps. A Good Samaritan had turned her in for stealing rainwater. She had been collecting it in buckets, and then used a solar still to extract the evaporite. The result was drinkable water.

It was a crime, sure, but she was already in the system. The report had cost someone a hundred caps to get, but you couldn't make a dime on it.

She couldn't afford an attorney, so obviously she didn't deserve one. Still, she seemed to argue the point.

Sarah Aisling: Rainwater belongs to all of us. That Ackerman Brothers has a slip of paper saying it is theirs does not—

Judge: It's not the paper, it's the effort. They spend a fortune protecting the environment from pollution and abuse so they can sell a quality product. Every cup you take out of the air is a cup less they can harvest, and a cup less you buy. You're looting them, their stockholders, colleagues, even their paying customers who have to make up the difference in higher prices. You really need to hire a defense to explain—

Sarah Aisling: I don't have the time, money or experience to find a good litigator, insure against a bad one, research that insurance, protect against insurance fraud, or learn all the applicable contracts myself.

Judge: You have futures available; you can sell against those to retain counsel.

Sarah Aisling: Who wants to invest in the futures of someone looking at jail time? My futures fell to pennies when I was charged.

Judge: And whose fault is that? Your futures are worthless because of your own actions. Don't use some sob story to mooch a litigator.

Sarah Aisling: But you're assuming I'm guilty.

Judge: They found six solar stills in your home!

Sarah Aisling: Of course, I was taking rainwater. But that doesn't mean I'm guilty.

Judge: Doesn't mean… It's the definition of guilty! Stop making—

Sarah Aisling: I can't defend against these charges because I can't afford a litigator. But I can't afford a litigator because I've been charged.

Judge: You should have had insurance against contract suits.

Sarah Aisling: I did.

Judge: So what's the problem?

Sarah Aisling: They canceled my insurance when I filed the claim.

Judge: So sue them!

Sarah Aisling: I can't, I don't have a litigator.

Judge: That's very cute, Mrs. Aisling. But again, it all comes back to you. Isn't it possible that you should have saved a bit more, been more careful with your money in case you needed it? Or—here's a novel idea—maybe you could have worked harder instead of plundering other people's work. If you're resourceful enough, there's always a way.

Sarah Aisling: That's a myth used by those with power to justify tyranny against those without it.

Judge: You could sell an organ if you had to.

Sarah Aisling: Why should I have to sell my futures or an organ to defend against charges that should never have been brought?

Judge: Honestly, I've never seen someone complain so much. You have a lot of excuses why this is everybody's fault but your own. That's how you get through life, isn't it? Excuse after excuse as to why your life is a failure.

Sarah Aisling: My life is not a failure.

Judge: One deserves precisely and exactly the defense one can afford, and you are a living testament to that. If you had spent less time complaining and stealing, and more time improving your value to the corporation, you would earn and deserve better representation.

I looked nervously around my cubicle. It was scandalous, rebellious. I was grinning from ear to ear—it was like watching a train wreck, seeing this woman square off with the judge. She already knew the outcome: she'd be fined, spend some time doing hard labor, maybe lose some rank. But she continued to argue. It was as if she wanted to be punished, thirsting to have more suffering heaped on her.

I logged in and purchased time with the full transcripts. As I read on I nearly fell out of my chair.

Sarah Aisling: Your Honor, I request that you recuse yourself.

Judge: On what grounds?

Sarah Aisling: You can't be impartial. You work for the people I am accused of stealing from.

Judge: That's what qualifies me. I understand the consequences of these crimes on the victims.

Sarah Aisling: I want a trial by jury.

Judge: Juries are a colossal waste of time. For every case you have to take twelve people off the street, explain the applicable contracts and procedures and how to make a fair decision. You get cases being decided by people with no court experience who just want to get out of there as fast as possible. It's the most inefficient system ever created! You're being tried by a certified and experienced judge, a judge of your peers.

I continued reading, heedless of the meter. I had never seen anything like it. She was contemptuous, dangerous, and didn't care in the slightest that the judge held her future in his hands. But he was so arrogant, so eager to exercise his power over her, that he missed something.

She was educated.

I would expect a LowCon to bemoan the "injustice" of the system. But Aisling wasn't angry, belligerent, or insulting. Her arguments were eloquent, coherent, and rehearsed well above her grade. She was talking about juries and property rights in ways nobody had taken seriously for centuries.

Who is this woman?

I plunged into her background, buying records from every source I could think of. She was born into a HighCon family that owned a software firm in Europa. She had been wealthier than I could ever hope to be, destined for Alpha-grade executive work, and had already contracted into a low Alpha by her early thirties.

But when she was thirty-five she began causing trouble for her corporation. She gave to charity, for starters (the Moral Hazard of which can't be underestimated. "Teach a man to fish," Linus would say, "and he can eat for life; but give a man a fish, and he doesn't need to learn anything"). I couldn't imagine the damage she wrought on corporate efficiency. She gave lectures on how some individual rights actually superseded corporate rights (this, despite the obvious and undeniable fact that corporations represent the welfare of millions of people).

I checked, but I didn't find any record of her ever being admitted into an insane asylum.

The only thing I did find was a story on a hotel fire. Hundreds died—in fact she was one of a handful of people to make it out alive. She changed after that.

It was compassion. The fire must have somehow infected her with it. By the time she downgraded to a low Delta she was booted out. We took her on as an Epsilon in a small subsidiary that rented out friends. By all accounts she was destitute, destroyed by her own ego and a desire to muddy the waters. She lived in LowSec with other Epsilons, Zetas and even people with no contract whatsoever (despicable NullCons).

I tried to track down her fortune. Some of it had been given away, some poured into the small, socialist, not-for-profit hospitals that exist in a few areas of Europa. All told I could account for about ninety percent of her wealth. The remaining ten percent, still a staggering amount of money, was unaccounted for. If she had spent it, where were the receipts? If she had given it away, where were the transaction records, who were the beneficiaries? No, she simply pulled it out of the bank and walked away with it.

And yet here she was, living in LowSec, refusing to get an advocate.

She still had the money. I knew it in my bones. She could afford an advocate, or a hundred; heck, she could just pay off the charges. She didn't do it because she thought she shouldn't have to.

This wasn't a colleague. This was a citizen.

I could write up a report on this that could pay off ten electric bills at almost any price! It might push me out of high Delta into a low Gamma contract, maybe even get me onto the ninth floor. I trembled, holding the paper in my hand. I shook so hard I thought I might tear it.

All I had to do was craft it right.

And craft it right, I did. I crafted a perception of her as a heretic, a purveyor of arcane and religious dogma—a belief that human beings had value above what they could produce. She was a pagan, a devil worshiper who abandoned morality, nature, and even common sense for a belief in the debunked "social contract," and in so doing undermined the good of all people cradled in the benevolent, invisible hand of the free market.

But that was just the beginning. Oh, I turned her into a seditionist, someone who proselytized and encouraged colleagues to abandon natural selection, competition, and evolution. She was, I wrote, "a citizen, a communist, extremely dangerous and likely representative of a much larger group of citizens who pose a serious threat to Ackerman." If Bernard could profit by taking a tiny issue and turning it into a catastrophe, then by God I would elevate her to the leader of a revolutionary movement.

When I finished, I had, simply put, the best report I had ever written. It was professional, concrete, not overly emotional—simple and to the point.

I leaned back in my chair and put the end of my glasses in my mouth. I chewed on them while I studied the thin blue piece of paper that had yielded a report that could so change my life.

What will this do to her?

The trouble she was in now was nothing compared to what might happen if I filed.

But that was my whole problem. I was always one bad utility bill away from bankruptcy. I had worked for Perception Management for years, but never adopted the ruthlessness Ackerman expected of me. It was the man who could most brutally stab a colleague in the back who was the richest. I wasn't there to protect her, to decide what was right or wrong. I was there to provide an indictment. Submitting the report was my job; defending herself from it was hers. If she failed, it wasn't my fault. Besides, my report would go through three hundred other offices for investigation or follow-up. I reported things; accuracy was another department. Heck, by this point I'd be liable if I *didn't* speak up.

I had been falling behind for a long time—not to people who worked harder, but those who did the job they were supposed to do—churn out reports to throw into the maw of Ackerman's perception machine.

And I had tired of the burden of ethics.

And, on some level, didn't she deserve it? She was so smug—the assumption that somehow *she* could lecture anyone on principles. Oh, how I'd love to be able to do that. But I didn't have rich parents who gave me the luxury of things to give up so that I could feel superior.

Hope is the slow death of man, and she spread it like a venereal disease: hope that there was something more to life than what you can produce. She shouldn't get to believe in that. Every child born to this world knows for certain that he or she is special, that they'll grow up to be a CEO, to become rich and famous, to change the world for the better. That is hope, and it's never true, and so we live lives of resentment and pain—inflicted on us by the gradual and repeated death of our dreams.

I tubed the report, shredded all my notes, and went to lunch.

3

The subway smelled like putrid milk, urine and moldy bread. It was sticky with substances I preferred remain a mystery, and the incessant squealing of brakes and rumbling of trains made me cringe. The tracks groaned and creaked under the weight of the steel hulks, and the tunnels were so small, the margins through them so thin, I thought that at any minute the coach would strike the wall, seize, and come to a grinding halt, entombing me so far below ground that any rescue would be uneconomical.

All this had very little to do with why I hated trains.

I hated them because they made a very good target—all those people crowded together. It was a LowCon way to travel. The stations increased in security the closer we got to Atlas Square, but passengers weren't fully screened until we got out. With every sudden jolt I'd wonder if my life was over, lost to a rival corp who considered a briefcase full of detonite a cheap and effective means of robbing Ackerman of some assets.

Arriving at Atlas Station, we were herded through x-ray machines, body scanners, and past bomb-sniffing dogs. That was where some suicide bomber would detonate, there in the crowd. I hadn't gotten my smoke in before coming, so I just closed my eyes and tried to relax, rubbing the referred pain out of my leg and wishing I had brought my pills as I was ushered through security.

I did, somehow and through the grace of God, arrive at Atlas Square. It was HighSec. In fact, short of the Galt, it had the highest security in the territory. It was the seat of Ackerman power and influence, the pinnacle of luxury and commerce, and a testament to the success of capitalism. A large rotunda sat in the middle, made of a beautifully trimmed lawn with *real* grass. It was surrounded by a U-shaped plaza made of two levels of HighCon shops and restaurants. In the center stood a towering marble statue of the god Atlas, on one knee, shrugging the whole world from his shoulders. The whole place was designed to make you feel important, as if you stood with the kings of men, that your very presence was enough to give your life meaning. You couldn't walk through the square without rolling your shoulders back, broadening your chest, and drawing your breath up from your shoes.

The only things that were allowed to wear were the stone slab sidewalks. They sagged slightly in the middle under the repeated pounding of millions of footfalls for hundreds of years, like a trickle of water that can, with enough time, cut through the strongest rock. The stones were original, never repaired or replaced, as if to say "Ackerman has existed since the dawn of time, and will continue to exist forever."

Around the square, past the markets on the far side, was an old intersection, from back in the days when cars were allowed to drive through. In the center on a small island sat a newsstand. It was pricy, but filled with literature from

Ackerman, our Karitzu, and even some competing corps. I used it in a pinch, or after lunch sometimes to show Linus that I wasn't afraid to spend a little money. The proprietor was a nice man who always seemed to know just what kind of stuff would help me out the most.

Past the newsstand, on the other side of the intersection, was the Café Americana. This nostalgic place honored capitalism in its infancy, back when it was regulated and looted by states and governments. It was long and slender, made up to look like a 1970's diner. Overstuffed red leather stools crowded the front and booths ran down the length. On the walls were posters of famous capitalists like John Rockefeller and Pablo Escobar, painted in bright reds and blues, with stars and sunbeams behind them.

It was one of the best coffee shops in the district, with a wide assortment of light fare. The prices were outrageous, even for a small sandwich, but that ensured a certain caliber of customer. I always bought lunch, and Linus' menu choices seemed calculated to be just enough to cause me pain, but not enough to humiliate, a mark he hit with frightening accuracy. But it was good for me to have a mentor and to be seen rubbing shoulders with a colleague of his stature.

Normally the place was quiet, exclusive—never more than half-full. But on that morning it was packed, and a long line had formed out the front. Thankfully, Linus was sitting on a stool in the front corner, quietly reading *The Arbitrage Daily Journal*. An empty seat waited beside him. Nobody asked him about it, and when someone bumped it or his table, he would simply look over his half-frame wire reading glasses and check that nothing had spilled.

"Sorry I'm late," I said.

Linus looked over the rim of his glasses, dubiously, as if I had arrived exactly when he had expected.

"Never apologize," he commanded, quietly. He raised his arm grandly and thrust it out, exposing his watch in a deliberate stroke. Then he drew his eyes from me to the timepiece. He turned back to his magazine. "For anything."

Linus Cabal was built like a tank. He had played rugby at school, and leveraged his skills into a scholarship at François Quesnay, one of the most prestigious universities in the territory. For most athletes their intellectual careers ended there. But while he ranked third in the sport, he studied too, and graduated fifth in a class of eight hundred. The players called him a nerd who didn't have the guts to dedicate himself to the sport. The academics called him a muscle-head who could have been valedictorian if he had gotten serious.

But when the recruiters came, he told the firms that he hated the tedium of corporate life, and he told the leagues that he was terrified of getting an injury. The ensuing bidding war over his talents landed him a position in Ackerman's Arbitrage division at the highest starting salary of any colleague on record, almost double what his valedictorian got.

"Business is war," Linus would say, "and all war is based on deception."

I wondered, casually, if Linus could tell the difference between the truth and a lie anymore, or if, indeed, the distinction was even important to him.

In the war that is business, I wondered, *what new front has opened up to cause all this?*

"Why the crowd?" I asked.

Linus scowled and began stirring his coffee, as if the answer was so obvious it irritated him.

"Kabul Coffee is trying to set up their first shops in our territory. They snuck in under one of our free trade clauses with another Karitzu, so we have to let them in. They're opening up three shops in the capital next month. The first will be in the square by the end of next week. So Takashi ramped up production and cut prices. He's even tapped our bean reserves."

"He's lowering the price to drive Kabul out?"

Linus nodded. "They don't have Ackerman's deep pockets... We can run coffee at a loss for a decade without feeling a pinch."

"Isn't that..." I said hesitantly. I had started the sentence, and now I realized I would need to finish it. "... a subsidy?"

Linus pulled the spoon from his coffee and tossed it on the table.

"Honestly, Charles, sometimes I don't know why I meet with you. We're not socialists. Subsidizing an industry is obscene. It's illegal. Mr. Takashi would never do it. How on earth do you make your way through the world, even as a Delta, not understanding that? You're in Perception, for Christ's sake! If it looks like a subsidy to you, maybe you haven't thought it all the way through! To even suggest..."

He was right, of course. The suggestion itself was slander, probably actionable. Nobody in *that* café would have found a reward of five or ten caps worth the bother. Still, I shouldn't have said it.

Takashi was CEO, so he was perfect. This was not a point of pride, but a natural law. LowCons were a plague of biblical proportions on a corporation, tolerated only because their sheer numbers gave them considerable market power. A MidCon was simply someone who had learned either to screw up less, or to better demonstrate that his "mistakes" were actually the fault of those below him. Executives made nearly no mistakes, but rather spent the bulk of their time compensating for the ineptitude of their subordinates. The CEO, therefore, was perfect. If not, a superior colleague would have replaced him long ago.

When Takashi did appear to make a mistake, it was the good colleague who could trace the mistake back to its actual source, usually a lower-ranked worker. Being a MidCon, the blame often landed suspiciously close to my own desk, and I spent about half my day demonstrating how the problem was actually the fault of someone below *me*.

The real problem for Kabul was that, while Ackerman had started as a securities and futures brokerage firm, they soon began vertical expansion—making their own discount paper, coffee and snacks for their colleagues. Then they began selling on the open market, competing globally, and before long Ackerman had its own generic equivalents of nearly every product imaginable, from toilet paper to carburetors. When a higher quality or better value product came along, Ackerman just leveraged income from other products to wipe it out.

"If Kabul coffee does a better job, shouldn't they be allowed to compete on a level playing field?"

"Level playing field? How is that not code for socialism? Who's going to level the field? Who sets the rules, decides what makes it level? Who's going to enforce it without regulating the rest of us into the ground? Governments? Those old relics destroyed productivity. No, no, the only Objective way to do it is on the fly, between corporations. Fair is what the market decides or allows for, taking into account all of the forces that come to bear. If Kabul wants to try to take us on in Coffee, they can go right ahead. They've been cleaning up in Europa, and that's fine, but if they want to come here and start setting up shops, we'll defend ourselves. And when they set up in other territories in the Karitzu, we'll defend those too, because we're the biggest and strongest and that's our job, because pride is a commodity too. Nobody undermines our products in our own territory."

"If coffee is running at a loss—" I said.

"It's not a loss; it's an investment in our colleagues, our brand name and reputation, and in the future stability of the coffee market. It's long-term thinking. Only a Delta thinks it's a subsidy."

It was boredom, that force which pushes the state of equilibrium towards a greater and greater tolerance for risk, especially with other people's money.

I shifted uncomfortably, trying to curry favor with a new topic. I thought about telling him about my Aisling report. He'd have liked it. But I didn't say anything.

"I looked into broadening my portfolio."

"Good, it's about time you took my advice to heart. Who are you looking at?"

"Studio One. They're an entertainment and television production firm. They—"

"I know who they are, stay away from it."

"Well, it's a good company, I looked into it," I said. "A *lot* of people are buying it."

"Exactly why you need to avoid it. It's a solid company, sure. But the stock keeps going up even though they have the same shows as last year. It's a self-fulfilling prophecy. People think it's good so they buy it, driving up the price, which makes more people think it's good. The price skyrockets until finally someone points out that the emperor has no clothes. The stock plummets, and everyone is wiped out. It's a trend, that's all, and by the time you notice a trend it's too late to get in on it."

I didn't tell him that I had already bought the stock.

Linus looked at me wryly. "You need to play." he said.

He was referring, of course, to poker—that ubiquitous game synonymous with corporate living. On rare occasion you could find people who played it with cards—but at Ackerman we played the original Greek way, with dice. The stakes were decided up front. Then each player would throw six dice and keep what they rolled hidden from the others. The first player would bet on the minimum quantity of any given number on the table—for example two fives. Each subsequent player would have to raise the bet, either by raising the quantity of dice with that number, or the number itself (say two sixes, or three ones). This continued until someone called. Then everyone revealed their dice. If the total quantity of that number was equal to or lower than the bet, the better won; otherwise the caller did. Most everyone carried dice on them and played three or four games a day.

If Linus felt any emotion for anything at all it was a love of poker. He denied it, but he had recorded every televised game—every match, every championship—for the last twenty years. He watched them, over and over again—studying faces, tells, and dice probabilities. He talked about how he'd spend thousands of caps in games he had no intention of winning, just to learn people's tells and get them later when the stakes were higher.

"My boss comes up to me..." Linus once recalled. He loved telling stories, old fables and personal vignettes. The grand and royal nature of storytelling attracted him to it, playing to his dramatic tendencies and delicate flourish. "He waited until I was in the middle of the trading floor giving my morning briefing. I had all of my subordinates around me, and he threw down. Challenged me to a game for a hundred thousand caps."

"So you beat him?" I had asked.

"Couldn't. If I beat him publicly, he'd destroy me for it."

"So you refused to play?"

"Couldn't. If I didn't play, I'd be seen as a coward to my subs. They'd all start jumping ship to work for someone with balls—someone like him. Make no mistake, this wasn't a game, it was extortion."

"So what did you do?"

"I laughed at him, told him a hundred thousand was a waste of time. I said if he was serious, I'd play for a million."

"You could afford that?"

"Doesn't matter. The question was, could he? He blew the whole thing off as a joke and walked away."

"He brushed it off?"

"It is, more often than not, the person willing to risk the most—even his own utter ruin—who wins."

"So you got out of playing him?"

Linus sighed. "No, Charles. What I'm saying is that I beat him before the game even started."

He told that story often, and whenever he thought I was missing a valuable corporate lesson, Linus insisted we play. That's all poker was: an exercise in lying.

I gave myself a half-hearted pat down and told him I didn't have any dice on me.

"We don't need dice," he said, pulling out a bill from his pocket. "We can just use caps. Every bill has a twelve-digit serial number on it. There are twice as many numbers and they range from zero to nine so it's a little harder than dice, but it's the exact same thing."

I failed to see how twice as many numbers was "the exact same thing."

"Well, I haven't studied the probabilities."

"The probabilities are irrelevant. Play the person, not the numbers. Lie to me, use your bets as a weapon."

"You'd have me at a terrible disadvantage."

"Then next time don't get caught without dice."

I stood there, frantically trying to come up with another excuse not to play. He pulled a cap from his pocket, memorized the numbers in a single pass, and then held it to his chest.

"Three sevens," he said.

I hated the game, which was no doubt why he wanted to play.

"If you'd like, we can wager today's lunch."

I had no excuses left. I pulled out a cap and read the serial numbers. Most were different, only a few repeats and no more than two of any number. It was a poor hand, which meant the blessing of a quick game. His face was expressionless, but his eyes shone with the certainty of an outcome I didn't dispute.

I had two eights. Linus probably had at least one, so I called out "Three eights" and prayed he'd call right then and there.

"Four Twos," he said. He'd calculated his second bet long before I had even given my first.

I hated poker. I hated playing it, hated people who liked it, hated the fact that everyone was playing it all the time. It was like a joke that everybody got but me, one I had long given up asking people to explain. Even Bernard, who lost more than I did, seemed to enjoy it.

Maybe I've been going about this all wrong. I know Linus. I can play the man and not the dice. He's proud—so proud that he might brush it off if I won, but he'd never play me again. Even he gets a bad throw on occasion. Win this, and I'll never have to do this silly exercise again.

I began thinking about how to take what I knew about Linus and leverage it into a victory. I had to do something unexpected, that was the key. I could bet outrageously high, but that had the downside of being unexpected for a reason—it was supremely stupid. No, I'd need to bid the highest number I could get away with, something that would force him to bid numbers higher than he could possibly have, and then I could call him.

But I didn't have anything myself, no real numbers to work with. But therein, I realized, lay the opportunity. I'd bid outside the range of what I actually had, but inside the range of what was likely—something I should have, but didn't.

"Four sevens," I said confidently.

"You're a liar," called Linus. He placed his bill face down on the table and went back to reading his journal.

His cap had exactly three sevens on it. If I had had even a single seven, I'd have won the match. And since I always paid for the meals, there hadn't been anything at stake. There was nothing to lose, and somehow I'd lost anyway.

"Don't worry about it," Linus said, dismissively waving his hand. "I'll pay for the meal."

"No, no, of course not," I said. "All my bets are good."

I had stopped carrying poker dice for this very reason. Now I'd have to stop carrying cash too.

"You know," Linus said, folding his paper and putting it on the table, "I saw your wife in the dailies again. It was buried in the back, a minor thing, but she was there. Did you know?"

"No," I lied.

"That's three ranks she's lost in four weeks. That makes her... what? A Delta five? Maybe even four? Another couple of weeks of this and they'll downgrade her contract. You'll be married to an Epsilon, Charles, a *LowCon*," he said, emphasizing every syllable.

I didn't know why I hadn't done anything about it. I was loath to talk about it, though.

"You're compassionate. That's the problem, Charles."

"I'm not!" I said.

"Generous, maybe?"

"What the hell!" I shouted. "Why, just this morning I—"

"Yes?"

"Nothing."

"You are compassionate," he said. "Get over it. I've seen it in you before. It's why you can't climb higher than Delta. It gets really bad around the executions. Tell me, do they bother you at all?"

"Bother me? Of course not!" I snapped. "These people all stole from Ackerman; they're all thieves and looters, and Ackerman has every right to recoup their losses."

"No, Charles. It's not a right. It's an obligation. Ackerman is duty-bound to its shareholders and to every colleague in the firm to raise profits as high as possible. These executions provide ad revenue, reclamation income, ticket sales, and deterrence against other violates. They're a moral imperative."

"That's what I said."

"No, it's not," said Linus, taking a sip. "You think we should treat Kabul with kid gloves? You don't want to confront your wife? You're thinking like a child. Compassion isn't natural, it certainly isn't economical, and it's the antithesis of capitalism."

"I know that!" I said.

"Do you? A child looks at your wife and says 'Oh, poor her. She's having a hard time; I wish her life were easier.' An adult says, 'This is life, and I'm accountable for myself.' A child sacrifices himself for a friend; an adult realizes when the friend is hurting him. She's hurting you, Charles; this is self-defense, here. It's is a business arrangement. If she has half a brain in that skull of hers, she won't take it personally. But if she did, it wouldn't be your fault."

She probably wouldn't take it personally. Maybe that was part of why I hadn't left her.

Lunch had turned out to be a disaster, no two ways about it. Despite how much I paid for his mentorship, he had never had that much respect for me, and I wondered why he continued to see me.

"You know," he said, "there was once a farmer living in China...."

Oh boy... a fable.

"One day the farmer's only horse broke free and ran away," he continued. "His family was on the brink of starvation. The villagers tried to console him, but he would only say 'it could be a good thing, it could be a bad thing.'

"The next day his horse came back, and brought with it ten more horses. Now he was the richest man in the village. They tried to congratulate him, but he would only say, 'It could be a good thing, it could be a bad thing.'

"Weeks later the farmer's son was thrown from one of the new horses. His back was broken and he was paralyzed from the waist down. Still, all the farmer would say was 'it could be a good thing, it could be a bad thing.'

"The next year their nation went to war. All of the tribe's young men were conscripted. They all died, except the farmer's son, who couldn't go. And when the envious villagers told him how lucky he was to still have a son, he said 'it could be a good thing, or it could be a bad thing.'"

Linus appeared to think the moral was obvious, but I didn't see it.

"You need to understand this, Charles, because it's very important. Every act, every single human act, has infinite levels of regression—of both good and bad consequences. When somebody says something is 'good' or 'bad' they are simply presenting you with whatever set of consequences they find matches the beliefs they *already* hold.

"But there is no such thing as good or bad; they're illusions, words, arbitrary slices of time engineered to elicit a sympathetic response. Outside of that slice, they don't exist. There is no difference between the saint who gives food to starving children and the worker who operates the gas chamber to kill them, except that one is making money and the other is losing it. These are the Objective realities Zino argued for."

"That's not in the Bible."

"It's the only logical inference from her work."

"If that's true," I said, "why bother being 'good' to the Corporation?"

It was a stupid thing to say. I regretted it the moment I said it. But I felt a sense of relief, as if I had loosed the elephant in the room.

Linus' eyes bulged. "Because..." he whispered, leaning in, "they're the only thing keeping you alive. How long do you think you'd last out there without your corporate contract? Rest assured, I have never done an unselfish thing in my whole life. I am loyal because I need powerful friends, and Ackerman is the best. You don't think I get offers from other corps? You don't think I'm in high demand? I don't ever even think about it. I'm loyal to the corp because it's good to me, because it's in *my* best interest to be."

I felt an overwhelming sense of emptiness. Linus could easily be a Retention agent, which would explain his interest in me. Even if he wasn't, any number of agents might be lunching in the café. I didn't care. Sarah Aisling stood up to a judge. I couldn't even stand up against a game of poker.

"All living creatures care about their own survival—at least all the moral ones."

I gave my coffee a half-hearted stir.

"Leave her…" He said in a commanding whisper.

"I've thought about it," I said, in a last-ditch effort to placate my colleague. "But the cost is way too high, and I'm sure she'll turn herself around. She's very—"

He slammed his hand down on the table in disgust. "You see, Charles, that's Delta level thinking right there. You won't be promoted if you don't start to think long-term. It'll cost you 20k to get a divorce, but if you turn around and marry a rising star—a high Delta or low Gamma, you can get that money back in three or four years. You're Gamma-level material, maybe even Beta-grade," he said. "Well, at the very least you could get Gamma. You just don't have the motivation, and honestly I have no idea why not. You probably think too much. But this 'oh, she's a real go getter; this is just a phase; oh, she'll turn it around' wishful thinking is absolute garbage. It's beneath you; I have no idea why you entertain it."

A reliable divorce was closer to one hundred twenty-five thousand caps. I couldn't imagine that he himself could get one for much less. But we were playing poker now, as we always did. And, as always, he could see all the dice on the table.

4

I stood in the undulating subway car, thinking about Sarah Aisling. She was an aberration, a genetic defect. She could have gotten her life back but instead squared off with the judge. What must have happened to her? What secrets did she think she knew that caused her to choose self-expression over self-preservation? She probably didn't like the executions any more than I did, but *she* wouldn't hesitate to say so. And besides the vigor of her conviction was the quality of her arguments. She had spent a lot of time thinking against the corporate structure. Aisling wasn't the first socialist I had ever seen or heard of, not the first lunatic or atheist either. But that anybody so educated could be so liberal—it confounded me.

When I returned to work I found nearly everybody out on the field. The building was cordoned off by officers and tactical teams, and colleagues were all bouncing off each other in a frenzy of chatter. Along a side street stood ambulances and police cruisers. A reconstruction team, carrying body bags, was just coming out of the building.

"Charles!"

Thane Corbett ran up to me, eager for a gratuity for being the first to fill me in. He was a sculpted, athletic black man, with a serious face and a very thin goatee. He was without a doubt one of the smartest people on the seventh floor. He exuded success. This, of course, ruined his career. Nobody likes success. Successful people remind you of your own failings, they highlight (to both you and your boss) what you're doing wrong and how easy it is to do the job right. They increase competition and expectations, both of which make your life harder. No, Corbett was chained to the seventh floor, and for all his vaunted intelligence, he'd never figure out why.

"Thank God you're back. Have you heard?"

I shook my head and handed him five caps.

"One of the guards snapped," he said. "He went on a killing spree, up on the second floor."

A pain shot through my chest and my throat felt thick. I already knew who did it.

"It was hilarious! You know, there was actually an executive doing an inspection there," he laughed. "Can you imagine that, if some executive was wiped out by a simple random act of violence? Classic!"

"So what happened?" I asked as casually as I could.

"Nothing, he shot some people, but security closed in and he killed himself. Obviously they won't let us do the perception on this one, but there's a pool going. It's ten caps to get in. That new guy, Collin, thinks that they'll be so thrilled the executive survived that security will get a commendation. Can you believe it? I'm going to love taking his money from him. Honestly, I'm going to find a way to destroy that naive little noob before the year is out. I'm gonna own him."

I watched the body bags being carted carelessly away. I didn't feel anything for my murdered colleagues. I just felt sorry for Simon, and wondered which bag he was in.

"They'll fine half our officers for not stopping it sooner, the duty officer for not predicting this, human resources for not preventing it. It'll be a blood bath... pardon the pun."

My father had been an accountant. The theory of accounting is that it's the accurate tracking of money. The practice was about making the books look as attractive to investors and stockholders as possible. He could have refused to do it on moral grounds, but there were ten other accountants willing to take his place, and he had a family to feed. He worked at a small firm that reclamated plastics. Most of the people there worked sixteen to eighteen hours a day; they all shared bunks on site. Suicide was a problem, so the firm installed bars in the windows and netting between buildings to protect their assets. One day my father fell into one of the processing vats. He shouldn't have been up there, so his insurance didn't pay out. My mother argued with them; we needed the money to live. But they said it was a suicide and wouldn't pay us. And we both knew they were right.

As Corbett calculated the odds and permutations of perception, I wondered why I didn't see it coming. I had seen him that morning in the lobby, "reading" his book. His condition should have been obvious.

You saw it. Don't pretend you didn't. And don't pretend you don't get it. Whatever it was that drove Simon to that most un-natural of acts, it's creeping up on you too. Is that why you're asking Linus about subsidies and loyalties? Retention will find out sooner or later. Are you trying to work your neck into a noose?

Ackerman Employee Retention was the most dangerous division you could encounter—even talking about them was risky. They had the right to blackmail, murder, extort, and survey nearly anyone in order to ensure colleagues' fidelity to Ackerman. And Retention wasn't simply reactive, they were proactive. They set up phony job offers from other corps, bribes and blackmail attempts, all to test loyalty. Their budget was classified, but they were the highest earning division in the corp, and reported directly to Takashi himself. Purportedly they had sleeper agents in every division, and I certainly didn't doubt it.

"What's wrong, man?" Corbett said. "Hey, relax. We haven't had one of these in a couple years. We were due. They had three up in Occam last year alone."

Someone will get me. Maybe it'll be Corbett, or Linus, or Bernard. Leoben the stabber would be a good bet, or one of my twenty other supervisors. Doesn't matter. Simon just had enough. Aisling too—she had gone on strike, just pulled her money and her effort out of the system.

"Simon..." I whispered.

"Simon, that's right. How'd you know?"

I had said his name aloud. "What?" I asked, playing for time.

"Simon. You knew the guard's name?"

"Well, yeah, he was the morning guy at the desk, we all knew him."

"No," said Corbett, his eyes widening with the prospect of financial gain, "you knew he was going to do this!"

I had thought Corbett might get me, but I certainly didn't think it would be today.

"Don't be silly," I laughed. "I mean, sure, there was something wrong with him. Anyone could see that. I reported my concerns to Human Resources nearly six weeks ago. I had no idea he was still a danger. Heads are going to roll in HR when I find out why they didn't do something about him."

He eyed me suspiciously. Heck, it would be his word against mine. If he was smart, he'd tell someone that I helped Simon plan the attack. Then I'm on defense, and Ackerman would believe whomever it wanted. Hell, let's be honest, since the truth of things can never be known anyway, they'd go with whatever was more profitable.

He smiled a touch out of the corner of his mouth. I didn't know if he was satisfied with my answer or not, but he grinned and shook his head. "Yep, a lot of money can change hands over this one. The only real losers are going to be our insurance. Simon was young; his futures had some value, even for an Epsilon."

I nodded as I wondered how much it might cost me to plant a backdated complaint about Simon to HR. It'd cost a lot more now that he was dead. It might be enough just to pay HR to keep an eye out for Corbett, in case he came checking into my story.

"And another thing," Corbett said, "your partner is after me again."

"Stop saying he's my partner. I just rent him half my cubicle. I've got no more control over him than you do."

The tactical teams packed up, and people were slowly being let back into the building.

"Increase his rent."

"If I do, he may split, and I need his share."

"Damn it, ever since Gollum got mugged he's done nothing but whine, and complain, and try to get sympathy for it. It's been three weeks now and he still chases me around asking for a ride, saying he's too scared of the subway. I've got better things to do than to dodge him all day."

"So just say no."

"Are you kidding? This is a people business. The word 'no' shouldn't even be in your vocabulary; it just upsets people. It's much better just to avoid him entirely."

"Charge him more for the trouble," I suggested.

"I charge him plenty. He offers me fifteen or twenty caps a ride. The problem is that by the time we get there he tells me he only has six on him, or his ledger is on the fritz, or his transfer fees have just skyrocketed so he'll just pay me one lump sum at the end of the month. Then I'm on the hook for more rides, because if I piss him off too much I won't see a dime. It would cost me at least a hundred caps just to file a breach of contract against him, and he knows it."

"Diabolical..."

"Why don't *you* get a car?" Corbett asked.

"We've got one, but Beatrice usually takes it. Besides, it's not worth the cost of diesel, the maintenance, overhead..."

"It's not the overhead," Corbett said, "but freeloaders and moochers trying to bum a ride off me."

"Well, that's overhead. Just take a bike, a lot less trouble."

"To work? My God, what if someone sees me? Nobody will take you seriously if they don't think you earn enough to drive. Besides, I've seen your bike... I choose life. You know, I'll bet you Susan down in accounting paid for it..."

"My bike?"

"No, the mugging. Bernard's mugging."

"You don't think it was random?"

"No chance. Nobody likes him, and he's been trying to buy his way into her bed for months. I'm thinking of getting a pool together, see if we can't get him taken care of. It'd be expensive, the guys upstairs like him and for some reason his stocks actually have some value. Still, there's got to be a way."

I shrugged. Corbett had always been after Bernard, but he appeared to have put some thought into this.

"Maybe another mugging and he'll go the way of Simon," he said.

"He's not Simon."

"There's got to be a way to hurt him."

"Hurt him bad enough, someone will get you for it."

He looked at me meanly. "Don't tell me things I already know."

"Okay."

"Some reason you protecting him?"

"I told you, I need his half of the rent."

"All right, I'm going back inside. Got to feed the beast."

I nodded. "So you don't want him to know I saw you?"

Corbett pursed his lips. He pulled my five caps back out of his pocket and slammed them back into my hand. Then he went back inside. I watched the last of the bodies carted away, and then followed after him.

5

The action on the seventh floor was winding down for the day. Most of the people who weren't working through the night had gone home a little early to watch the hangings. Corbett was hiding in my office, since that was probably the last place Bernard would look for him.

"You know, Linda wants to have kids," Corbett said.

"Linda? Do you want 'em?"

"Do you know how much they cost? The license alone is about twenty grand. And sure, if you sell their futures right, it's income for life, but it takes forever to just break even. No, there are faster ways of making money. Besides, look at Eric."

I looked into the hallway. Number 721 was still on. He hadn't even closed the curtains.

"He still here?"

"He's always here. He sleeps in there now, has to."

"He works harder than all of us." I said.

"Lot of good it'll do him."

I nodded.

Eric Forestall was in a lot of trouble. His parents chose not to sell his futures—they kept them safe for him till he was eighteen. When he got them, he went wild, selling them for cars, women and liquor. Within six months he had sold them all, and had nothing left but creditors expecting dividends.

"Serves the parents right, weakening a kid by not selling him outright," Corbett said. "Never learned to handle money. Talk about Moral Hazard."

The boy's futures had plummeted, and now he was working night and day just to try to stay ahead of it. The lower they got, the more likely someone would simply reclamate him and be done with it. Every penny he made went to keeping himself out of the lye vats for one more day.

"You know," shouted Corbett, "I hear they like to toss you into the vats while you're still alive. It makes the best soap!"

There was no reply.

"Think he heard me?"

I shrugged. That notion was an old wives tale, something parents told their kids to get them to behave. It wasn't true (well, at least I think it wasn't. I honestly don't know much about the process).

"Well, when they take him, it'll be one more cubicle free. Can only help prices. That'll be Collin in a year or two..."

At home I found Beatrice curled up on the floor in front of the television, a bowl of popcorn, some chips, and a remote office terminal in front of her. The poker championship was coming down to the last few throws, but she wasn't giddy because of the game.

Already she was fantasizing about the executions, about each person begging for their lives, truly broken and in denial before the drop. They would realize their sins and repent, right before succumbing to the inevitable hand of justice. She delighted in watching them pay, as if every one of them had committed their crimes against her personally. Death sports—gladiators paid to put their lives on the line—never amused her. No, it was the executions or nothing. She once told me that she imagined them, dangling helplessly against the rope, willing to trade anything they ever had, anything they ever could have, for a second chance, but finding that no matter how much they wished, Ackerman's wrath would always win out. She loved justice.

The stadium was packed with Alphas, most of whom paid as much as one hundred thousand caps a head to watch live. Execution parties were common—Corbett had his own every month (I usually paid him a few caps not to be insulted by my absence. Watching people die was a bit like watching pornography, it never did strike me as a group activity). My neighbor always had friends over to watch, too. We could hear the cheering through the walls with the crack of each broken neck, and the shouting of bets—like at a derby—when someone choked against the rope. We hardly needed our own television.

Beatrice never attended the parties either. She called them "debauched," but really she just became enraged when she saw people enjoying the show. Who were they to be as offended by criminal behavior as she was?

"Running late?" I asked.

"Yeah," she sighed, sending off another report. "Jennings is taking forever to call this last guy."

Susan Jennings. Even I knew that name. Everyone knew *that* name. She was the greatest poker player in the world. Linus would never admit it, but he idolized her. When she lost a game, he bragged about her genius, throwing a couple matches a season to confuse competitors looking for tells or an angle on her strategy. When she lost last year's championship, he pronounced it decisive proof of her brilliance—a gambit for dominating the league in years to come.

What do you feel, I wondered as I pulled out a few individually wrapped shots of whisky from the fridge, when your execution is delayed because the previous show ran long?

I downed my first shot.

Suddenly Bea jumped to her feet. "I almost forgot! Guess what I got you!" she said, handing me a thin brown paper bag. "A colleague of mine recommended this. The reviews were all glowing."

Inside was a pornographic magazine; on the cover a picture of a naked woman bent over a sawhorse, a man with a whip behind her.

"Oh, my!" I exclaimed. "Yes, that does look good."

"All the men on my floor say it's the best. They're *always* talking about it. Anyways, I don't know how long it's been... well, how long since you... anyways, I thought you might enjoy this. I heard that they use real leather whips."

"No."

"They do. And this cost only cost five caps!"

"Five? Wow, that is surprising. It's higher quality than most stuff you'd find."

"My colleagues know what they're talking about. I guess there are a few scenes of men with men in there. I don't know if that's your thing. You can ignore those pages, or give them a try, whatever you want. I can leave for a little while after the show, give you some privacy."

I nodded. "Very thoughtful, thank you. Did you bill me for this?"

"It's already on your ledger."

"Oh, thank you. No, this is really nice, thanks. I'll be sure to look it over after the show."

I didn't know what else to say. If it really cost only five caps, then maybe it was a good deal, even if it wasn't a style or brand I liked. But in all the time I had been married to Beatrice, "bargains" like this came along only after a fight, or as a prelude to one.

She sat back down. The whisky made me feel warm, and my mind began to wander.

No debt... His work record was fine. He'd never have made Alpha, but that was true of most people. Simon had a steady and reliable job. And Aisling, throwing her life away for no reason. Forestall will be next, but at least he'd have an excuse. It's a rash of suicides, a cluster. Maybe the hormone content of the water is off or something.

I downed a second shot.

The apartment shook with the stamping of feet as Jennings destroyed her last opponent. Bea gave a petite, joyous clap of her hands.

"Are they killing anyone special today?" I asked. I didn't care. In fact, I'd rather not have known.

"Malcolm Evans, the spy!" she said with glee. "They'll probably make him the last one."

I shuddered.

"Aren't you excited?" she grinned.

Evans was a Beta, a good one. He had been well respected, efficient and avaricious. He worked in Acquisitions, luring disgruntled or undervalued employees from competing corps (even from our own Karitzu, if he could get away with it), and obtaining insider information from people willing to sell it.

The job was as dangerous a one as you could get. Enemy Retention programs were ruthlessly trying to stop you, feeding you disinformation while trying to trick you into giving up your own secrets.

Evans had been doing a great job, but he suffered from a disease that plagues most colleagues at one point or another: he thought he wasn't being paid enough. He was approached by a man pretending to be a Hiragana Acquisitions agent. He flattered Evans, told him that Ackerman didn't appreciate him enough or recognize his genius, and that a smaller corp like Hiragana understood his needs much better.

Evans didn't buy it on the first pitch. He had been dissatisfied with Ackerman, for sure, but they probably knew it. He made the guy for a Retention agent right away. But, like any good Acquisitions operative, Evans kept pretending to be interested, mining for information.

Then the agent offered to have a meeting at Hiragana's headquarters, and Evans' interest was aroused. He figured that not even the best Ackerman Retention agents could ever set up a sting from the main offices of a hated rival like Hiragana. He researched the people he'd meet with, the contracts he'd sign—everything was on the up-and-up. They'd offered him more money than he'd ever make at Ackerman, a position as an executive running their Acquisition Department, and a guarantee against Ackerman retaliation.

He signed the contract and they arrested him on the spot.

He had been right, of course. Hiragana would never have let Ackerman do an operation from their own HQ. But Retention had blackmailed a bunch of Hiragana officers and promised to let them off the hook if they set up and executed the sting themselves. They held dozens of meetings throughout the day, all with real Hiragana employees and Hiragana branded contracts. By the time it was over, seventeen colleagues were in the hands of Ackerman Retention.

But that was just the start. Retention offered Evans a deal—pay off some of your debt by becoming a stabber. Rat out your colleagues, and maybe we'll let you live. For four months he tried. He asked co-workers questions about their work habits, personal lives, pet projects—all the while trying to find something he could use to gain leverage. But he was desperate and clumsy, they all suspected him right out of the gate. He started gathering whatever intelligence he could, turning in confidential documents to help Retention in old cases or to start new ones. They took it all, and then added espionage and spying to his list of charges.

That's the real reason the hangings were so popular. Like watching a car wreck, it was conclusive proof that, no matter how badly you screwed up your life, somebody else had done it worse.

The television screen faded out. The sound of booming Takio drums filled the air and the spotlights came into view. In the sky was a blast of fireworks, and the stadium lit up. Beatrice squealed as the ceremonies began.

For the last fifteen years or so the ceremonies had been hosted by the same three pundits. Paul and Steve were the youngest. Paul was dark-haired, athletic, with an air of intellectualism about him. Steve, on the other hand, was a gentle giant, bigger even than Linus, with a broad chiseled chest, but wearing a finely tailored suit that made him look nicely kempt.

The third commentator was Alice. She was vacuous and plain-looking. She wore a tan skirt and coat over an off-white blouse, and she was showing every one of her fifty-five years.

"Oh, that woman. She is horrible. They shouldn't ever put her in front of a camera, don't you think?" Beatrice said. "They should let me produce the show. I'd get someone with looks in there, attract more men. She's stupid, too. Producers don't know anything these days. Don't you think I could do a better job? You know I could! I'd clean house. I'd fire the whole production staff, starting with her. Keep Paul and Steve, those two are awesome!"

The anchors reviewed the night's line-up. Alice would invariably say a nice thing or two about each of the condemned before being trounced by her co-hosts. She would point out how maybe the crimes weren't as bad as the media made them out to be, or that maybe the courts or police hadn't treated them fairly. Every time—by a revolving mixture of a cold recitation of the facts, persuasion, and ridicule—she would come around.

"And then there's the main event, Malcolm Evans!" said Steve.

"Oh," said Alice, excitedly. "He's the Acquisitions one?"

"That's right, Alice!" said Paul. "The worst of the bunch!"

"Well, you know," she said flippantly, "I know he's a bad guy and all. But do you really think he's guilty of ALL of the charges?"

"Here we go…" moaned Steve.

"I'm just saying, espionage? I know he tried to get out of his contract. But once they had him on that, it looks a lot like it was Retention that blackmailed him into committing more crimes. They're the ones who asked him to turn on his own colleagues."

"A crime is a crime," answered Paul.

"But Retention forced him to! He was just trying to save him—"

"Exactly!" said Steve. "He put his own needs ahead of the corporation. Nobody made him do anything. He could have just accepted responsibility for his crimes. But no, he tried to bribe Retention, save his own skin by throwing colleagues under the bus. Frankly, he's getting off easy."

"I suppose that's a good point." said Alice, as Bea snarled at her. "But if he wanted to leave the firm, shouldn't he have been free to go?"

"Of course Evans was free to go! He just needed to buy out his contract. And what's wrong with that? Ackerman invested a lot of money into him, it's only fair. And he was paid for his loyalty. He cashed those checks, and look what he did!"

Beatrice raveled her hands into her shirt and flexed in anger. "Yeah!" she cried. "My God, the communist! How do they let people like this on the show? She's been doing this for like a decade now! Honestly, does nobody at that network think? What I could do with the entire department if they let me manage it. They simply don't hire people with talent over there—they'd be intimidated by me, that's the problem!"

The first round of hangings began. The commentators bantered back and forth about the man's crimes. Alice, ever the voice of compassion, was universally rebuffed and overpowered by the weight of a single principle: the only chink in Ackerman's armor was disloyalty; Ackerman failed its colleagues only if its colleagues failed Ackerman.

The first few people were hanged. Beatrice grinned from ear to ear as each one dropped. When a neck broke, she let out a disappointed sigh. When it didn't, she watched them suffocate for minutes, squirming and clawing the noose for air.

"What made you think you could get away with it? It's your own damn fault!" she shouted at the television. "Honestly, idiots all of you! I mean nobody *wants* to hang their own colleagues, but when you behave like this... what did you think was going to happen?"

The gallows were iconic—every child knew what they were. Like the steps in Atlas Square, they were allowed to age. Once a golden oak color, they were a battered, weathered gray, cracking and splitting along every beam, yet somehow always up to the job.

They had an arcane and checkered history. A guard had once been careless with a prisoner and found himself tossed off the edge with a rope around his neck. A bloodstain still marked the fourth trap, the remaining ichor of Edgar Wellington, a horribly obese man whose head popped off when he fell. And let's not forget the bullet hole from a particularly incensed Alpha who took a shot at an extortionist, only to find himself hung three months later for the same crime.

For the first time in my life, I was part of that history. Sarah Aisling could end up there herself because of me.

No, your report isn't bad enough to send her there. The worst she'll get is hard labor.

But it wasn't true. If my superiors embellished as much as I had, if we all just kept heaping accusations on to her, of course she'd end up on the gallows. I knew that.

But it's not your fault. You can't control what other people do.

No, but I was responsible for my own actions. At some point we had abandoned responsibility and began fostering corruption in others so that we might shield ourselves from persecution by virtue of a common guilt. We did this in the name of profit, and we justified our crimes with the rationalization that, somewhere down the line, better people would safeguard our victims from us.

I wasn't a looter or a moocher. I wasn't a producer either. None of us were. We certainly weren't capitalists. We were pillagers.

Decency exists. That alone must make it important; even the great Darwin himself would say that. But we tried to cut decency out of others so as to lower the bar for ourselves.

We are relative creatures. The man who teaches his slaves to read is a saint in a world where slavery is legal, and a monster where it isn't. We aren't born knowing if we're good or bad. We decide by comparing ourselves to others—and by that yardstick it's no different to measure by our own successes than by our neighbors failures, save that it's easier to corrupt the neighbor.

A corporation wasn't a producer simply by virtue of being a corporation. Zino held up capitalists as the engines of the world. But those in her Bible succeeded because they were great people, not because they were capitalists. Not even she got that distinction.

Don't presume to know what Zino thought.

She was a person, just like me. And she said that A=A and that there was no God, and that to say so was Objective. But just as Objective was the inevitable conclusion that it must not be the crime that is wrong, but getting caught. Objectively, with the death of God, how could it be any other way? And with God dead, capitalism is as good a substitution as any.

Things can't really be this way.

I took another shot.

"Should you be drinking that much? Do you know how expensive those are?"

I didn't care. I didn't care how much they cost, or that they cost the same as it did to watch the executions in high definition. I didn't care that the lights were all on, or that she always drove the car.

I tried to figure how long I had to wait before I could take another shot without protest.

Linus often said that the executions were the greatest gift the corporation could give its colleagues. They were an expression of God and of the state of nature. It was a thinning of the herd, casting off the excess weight from a racecar, and allowed us all to better reap the benefits of our firm. But when I looked at these men and women dangling from ropes like carcasses in a butchery, all I could think was that it was the most unnatural thing I had ever seen.

The room began to spin. I could taste the whisky coming back up, and made a tumbling dash for the toilet. I lifted the seat and began to vomit.

"Darling, please try to keep it down in there," she said warmly. "I'm missing some of the commentary, and you know that's my favorite. And turn on the fan if you get a moment."

I heaved even more, dizzy and short of breath, clinging to the bowl. I begged for the surge to stop, but all I could do was brace myself for the next lurch.

"The fan, darling, remember the fan! You don't want to ruin the show!"

The retching finally stopped, and I slumped down, exhausted, hugging the john.

Finally I made my way to the sink, pulling the string to light the small bulb that hung from the ceiling.

The four walls made a cell—there was no better way to describe it. The gray paint, not retouched through four tenants, was cracking and chipping off. I placed my palm on the wall and rubbed, feeling the plaster break off and crumble under my hand. I turned on the water, splashed it on my face and rinsed out my mouth.

I heated up the water a bit, then washed the drywall dust from my hands—letting them lay there—bathing in the warmth and letting it circulate over the rest of my body.

Feeling rejuvenated, I dried them, the warmth retained. But I let the water run. I listened to the sound of it hitting the bowl, running down the drain, like the sound of fall leaves rustling in the wind.

I don't care that the water is running.

This is life, replied a lifetime of conditioning. It doesn't matter if you like it or not, it simply is the way things are. Competition is the only constant. Stars compete for fuel, plants for sunlight, and people for power. Beyond that there's no significance. It just is. Now turn the water off and get yourself together.

I don't care that the water is running.

I examined myself in the mirror. My face was weathered and bitter from years of endless conflict—with enemies, colleagues, neighbors, friends and my wife—with everyone I had ever met.

We aren't going to lose to socialism, to guilt or compassion. We've already lost. We've defeated ourselves, wearing ourselves to the nub. We aren't workers; we're fuel—fuel for a large machine that wants nothing more than to consume us for the lowest possible cost. I've been dying for a very, very long time, and I'm sick of it.

My conditioning spoke again, as the voice of reason. It said that life is the process of dying. What you're looking for, it said, is hope. Hope that there's more. Simon had hope once, but when he stared into the human soul and saw nothing but the abyss of our own nature staring back at him, he couldn't take it. You're stronger than he was. Just hold out, success is just around the corner. Somebody will see all the hard work you've put in, someone will notice that you're special. That's the promise of capitalism… just work.

I looked at my face: my eyes, nose and forehead. In my weekly baths I had never given my face much attention. So I washed it: behind and inside my ears, under the apple of my neck, and around my eyes. I hit every crevice, every wrinkle, and washed myself clean.

I lathered my face and ran the razor under the water. I hadn't given myself a proper shave in a while either. I went slowly, running the blade once, then twice, over the stubble, under the ears, below the chin, and across my cheeks. I looked at myself again, cleaner than I had ever been.

Competition exists in facets of life, but that doesn't make it the sum of life. You can see the world through rose-colored glasses, but that does not make the world rouge, even if you live a lifetime that way. Violence is the only possible conclusion to capitalism.

I wasn't a capitalist. I was a murderer. We were all murderers.

I grabbed a towel and dried my face. Then I left the bathroom and watched Bea for a few minutes. Not till the commercial did she notice me.

"There you are. Are you feeling better? Do you think maybe you used a bit too much water?"

I could see her—as clearly as Linus saw me. I was shocked that, as obvious as she was, I hadn't noticed her before.

"So, which corporation is it?"

"Which corporation is what?" she asked.

"Which corporation are you leaving Ackerman Brothers for?"

Beatrice turned white and looked at me in abject horror.

"Darling, where did you hear something like that from?"

"Nobody. Where are you going?"

"We both know you wouldn't think that on your own if someone hadn't suggested it to you. Today was one of your 'Linus' days, wasn't it? Does he think that I'm leaving?"

"I don't know what he thinks," I said. "It's what I think."

"Honey, what's this really about? You didn't like your magazine, is that it?"

"No."

"Is it the dailies? You saw I was in there, didn't you? I can explain—"

"I don't care about the dailies."

"Then why are you making a big deal about this?"

"You blame everyone for everything. If anything goes wrong in your life, you find someone to blame for it. But you've been losing rank for six months, and you haven't said a word. You've never complained, you've just taken it."

"I didn't want to trouble you..."

"You're screwing up on purpose, letting your rank fall. You're going to rank down till you drop into Epsilon grade, and then you'll buy out your contract and go somewhere else."

She looked at me gravely. "Charles," she said, "that would be illegal. I'm offended that you would even suggest...."

My whole life I wanted to have Linus' insight into the world. He was a sorcerer, a warrior monk and a commander of whole armies of colleagues, taking whatever he wanted. Beatrice was as transparent to me as a child who, with the strongest of convictions and certainties, blames a broken cookie jar on her imaginary friend. But I wasn't a wizard, anymore than Linus.

I raised my hand to interrupt her. "You don't need to answer. In fact, if you're going to keep lying, I prefer you don't. I was just curious."

"Charles, I've tried to be patient, but if you accuse me one more time," she said, "I will never forgive you. Someone is trying to turn you against me. Now, who said this?"

"I'm not going to turn you in," I said. "I'm not going to blackmail you. Really. I don't think I even care. I shouldn't have asked; it's really none of my business."

Satisfaction lit her eyes. "My god, you really do love me, don't you? You would suspect something like that, and yet you wouldn't.... You really aren't going to try to use this, are you?"

I was done profiting from the suffering of others.

"Oh my god, Charles, do you know how long I've waited for this moment? You're finally a part of this relationship. You're willing to see what I'm trying to do. Oh, I'm so glad you're on board. Ackerman has *never* acknowledged my gifts or what I can bring to the company. You know that. It's painfully clear."

She had been planning this move for a while.

"Studio One made an offer: Producer. They'll buy me out at eighty percent if I can get down to an Epsilon grade and make up the difference in escrow."

I had to struggle to keep myself from laughing. They were absolutely the flash in the pan that Linus said they were. And besides, in the eight years I had known Beatrice, I had never once found her to be entertaining.

"They only have five channels right now—but that just means more room to expand. They really see what I'm talking about; they know I can get their programming up to date. They've lost a lot of executives to defections and relocations, so they'll start me as a Gamma. It's a great opportunity."

Her life was over. It would end in a series of events determined even before they unfolded, like a mate in chess that's inevitable twelve moves away. I could read the necessary and inexorable steps yet to come.

Studio One's stocks were on fire and they were flush with money. But instead of saving it for the inevitable correction, they were spending it wildly. And the people who were most in a position to see disaster ahead—the executives—were all bailing out. When the company tanked, those who had stayed behind would blame the failure on the new blood. They weren't hiring a producer, they were hiring a scapegoat.

"They'll wipe you out."

"Who do you think you are?" she squawked. "You know, I thought you'd be happy for me. Jealousy is a very unattractive quality. They've already given us an apartment; I'd think you'd be grateful."

"I'm not going," I said.

Bea looked at me. "Is this because I didn't tell you? I had to keep this a secret; they wouldn't let me tell anyone. Besides, I didn't want you to worry. I was thinking of *you*."

"I'm not going."

"Don't be angry with me. I wanted to tell you."

"I'm not going."

"You know," she said, "you shouldn't make decisions when you're angry. Right? Why don't you sleep on it?"

"I'm not angry," I said. "I will not go. Not now, not ever."

"We'll talk about this when you're feeling more reasonable," she said.

"I'm not going."

"You're just feeling like you'll be less of a man because I'll be a Gamma and you won't. You're afraid that I'm going to think you're worthless. But you're my husband. What makes you have such a low opinion of me that you think I'd treat you like that? I'm a highly ethical colleague, you know that."

"You're right to leave, Bea. You've wanted this for a long time. Do what's best for you. But I'm not coming, and we'll both be happier for it."

"Oh, bless your heart," Beatrice said. "You think you're protecting me? You're too sweet. I want you to come. You don't need to act brave. You're so cute when you're like this."

"You're not listening."

She folded her arms. "Okay, now you're just being silly. Look, I was going to go by the place after the show. Come with me and check it out."

"No."

"How far do you want to take this, Charles? I'm perfectly happy to play games if you are. I can call your bluff. You think I should go? Is that what you want?" she raged.

"Yes. That's what I want."

She grabbed her coat. "I know you're just trying to be helpful, but we need to talk about your methods. I'll send a crew tomorrow to pick up my stuff. When you're ready to talk, give me a call."

She was Beatrice, the same as the day we had met. Our marriage should never have happened, and we had each been looking for the door for a while now. It just took this long for one of us to find it.

She left the apartment, which suddenly felt very quiet. I turned off the television. For the time being, my world didn't have to be anything more than those four corners. I didn't want to drink, but I couldn't think of anything else to do. I wasn't going to watch television. I didn't want to log in to or browse CentNet. I certainly didn't want to go to bed, since that only brought the next day at Ackerman that much closer. So I went into my bedroom, sat on my bed and cried.

6

By one A.M I still hadn't gotten off to sleep. I lay in bed, feeling more alive than I had in—well since I could remember. Sleeping, a practical necessity, wasn't going to happen.

I went to the toilet and flushed my remaining pills.

I never understood the world, or how people could feel so comfortable in it. Not until I had heard of Sarah Aisling did it even cross my mind that the problem might not be me.

Following up on her status would have been suspicious, and they probably wouldn't even have told me anything anyway. But with any luck her colleagues might know if she was all right. Heck with any luck, they might even be like her.

I sat down at my terminal and began browsing the social services directory. I found all kinds of adverts for every interest possible. Pleasuring services ran about fifty caps an hour. Abuse services (yelling, whipping and beating—all at the hands of an experienced professional) ran about eighty caps. To think that Beatrice had been doing it for free for almost a decade.

I wondered if I owed her back pay.

I finally found a friendship catalogue. The Ackerman-affiliated agencies were listed first. The ads were large and colorful, designed not only to attract the eye, but also to maximize download times and fees. The Karitzu ads came next. Finally I came upon the free trade section. Those ads were all plain and simple (to protect colleagues from excessive download costs).

Down near the bottom I found what I was looking for—a small yellow and black ad for the friendship agency where Sarah Aisling had worked. They didn't list a phone number, just an online order form. I requested a friend, to be delivered immediately. My ledger bleated, and the transaction was complete. A friend named "Katherine Wolfe" was on her way.

I began cleaning up the apartment—picking up the popcorn and potato chips, cleaning the dishes. It was a silly exercise; I had rented her, she'd be my friend no matter what the place looked like. I was in the process of moving the couch when she arrived.

I opened the door to find a tall, broad-shouldered woman standing in the pouring rain.

"Hi. Did you order a friend?" she asked.

Her hair was a long, fox red, and fell to just below her shoulders. Its sheen reminded me of a fresh cherry. Her face was warm, but most striking about her was that her eyes were each a different color—one was green, like fresh-cut grass, and the other was a light acorn.

"Yes," I said, ushering her in. "Are you my friend?"

"Yeah. My name is Katherine. You can call me Kate."

"I'm sorry about the rain," I said. "If I had any idea, I would have rented on some other day. Did you take the train?"

"No, a friend dropped me off."

Page 64

"A friend?"

She turned to a car idling under a lamp in the parking lot. An Arab woman with curly black hair sat in the driver's seat. Kate waved her off, and the woman waved back before driving away.

"Oh... a colleague. Well, still, you had to stand out there. I'm sorry."

"No, don't be silly."

I offered her a drink while I finished straightening up.

"Any cola would be fine," she said.

When she spoke, I found that I was staring directly at her eyes. The uniqueness drew me in and made her presence commanding. I didn't want to seem to be ogling, so I picked just one eye, the hazelnut, and looked at it when we spoke. Her voice was soft and gentle, and she seemed to have no awareness of the sway her eyes had over me.

"Whisky shots?"

She glanced suspiciously. "Aren't you the big spender this evening?"

I laughed with a boyish giggle. "Please, have some," I said, turning on the overhead light.

"You know I'm not an escort, right? That's another service."

"Oh, no, no! That's not it at all! I'm celebrating. I'll bet you get a lot of that, don't you? People hiring friends to try to get pleasuring services on the cheap."

"I would imagine. So what's the occasion?"

"Well, hiring a friend is an occasion all on its own, don't you think?"

"Sure."

"What do you mean," I asked, "'I would imagine.'"

"Huh?"

"I asked if people try to get pleasuring services on the cheap, and you said you'd imagine."

Kate gave a disappointed look. "Well, I'm... this is my first day working as a friend."

"Really?" I said. So we toasted providence. "Why the change in careers?"

"Oh, no, I've still got my old job. It's just—well, one of the agency's colleagues ran into a spot of trouble...."

Sarah Aisling. This was the closest I had ever been to someone I had reported, the first time I saw Aisling as a person. Those kids, with the broken soccer ball, whom I reported for slander. They had friends, family, parents who enjoyed watching their games. The difference between a name on a report and a person standing in front of you is the difference between seeing a sketch of two lovers, and the act of making love.

God help me, I had been reporting real people and somehow never knew it.

"... so I'm filling in."

I nodded. "My name is Thatcher, by the way."

"Thatcher? The invoice said your name is Charles."

"Charles? Oh my god, yes, that's my first name. I guess... well, in the corporation you go by the last name until you get to know someone."

"I like Charlie," she said.

"Charlie? My mother called me Charlie. My sister too."

"I like it."

"Thank you. A bit informal, though, don't you think?"

"Well, in LowSec we almost always go by first name. You hired a friend, so I thought... But whatever you prefer, Thatch—"

"No," I interrupted. "No, I think I do prefer Charlie."

We sat there quietly for a few moments, me with my first friend, and her with her first client.

"You have a sister?"

I nodded. "She's a sheet metal worker for a small corp on the west coast somewhere. At least she was. Mother worked there too. My dad died when I was seven. He was in a work camp for a while, and then went into accounting. Anyways..."

Page 66

I remembered a small shack we lived in before I was sold to Ackerman, just two years after my father died. I remembered the smell of old, soft wood, and the way you could look out through the cracks in the boards, and how the whole house creaked, even in breezes so small that you could only feel them by the hairs on your arm. The wood was weathered gray, the same as the gallows. I wondered why I had never remembered that before.

My mother *was* a metal stamper, I remembered clearly now. Every year or two she'd come home with one fewer fingers on her hand. After losing three and the tip of a fourth, they put her on polishing—she took a cut in pay and I was sold to make up the difference.

"Filling in?" I said, changing the subject.

"It's just for a week. I'm keeping my regular job."

"Two paychecks must be nice."

"Oh, I wish. I'm not getting paid for this."

I coughed up a swig of whisky on that. She apologized profusely for the shock. "She's a friend, Charlie. I'm filling in for a friend while she deals with her problems."

"You sublet her?"

"No," laughed Kate. "A compeer. You know, a friend in the archaic sense."

"Oh my god, really? What good is one of those?"

She shrugged. "Commercially? None, I suppose. But I offered to help out, we all did."

"That's not your job."

She shook her head. "It's nobody's job. That's why we did it."

I had done it—hit the mother-lode. She was a colleague—no, a friend—of Aisling's.

"Wow, a real flesh and blood communist."

"I'm not a communist, Charlie," she laughed. "God, no."

"You do things for free, isn't that the definition?"

"No, and I don't do *everything* for free, by any means. And I *do* get something out of helping out a friend, just nothing you can put on a balance sheet. We make each other laugh, we have fun together. When was the last time you laughed?" she asked.

"A colleague of mine went long on a thousand shares of Senya right before it went belly up. That was a riot."

"Ever laugh when it wasn't at the suffering of someone else?"

"Comedy is just tragedy from the other side of the street."

"Really? Have you ever had a colleague who would stand by you even if you couldn't make it worth their while?"

"That's socialism."

"I see..." she said. "You know, socialism is a very specific set of theories. Tossing out that word is a great way to kill an honest discussion, but having friends does not a socialist make."

"It's unnatural."

"Really?"

"Everybody is selfish. We all want money, power. People who deny that are just afraid to compete or are just too lazy," I said, futilely.

"And people who say that are simply trying to justify their participation in a vicious system. You need money, sure, you can't live without it. But happiness is a need too, Charlie, not much point in living without that. Tell me, are you happy?"

"Nobody's happy."

"Nobody *you know* is happy. They all have to buy their lovers. They compete like a hamster on a wheel—every step they take does nothing more than bring the next one closer. Nobody's the best, someone is always coming up right behind you, so there's always further to run. You compete, you guard yourself against everyone you meet, and then you die. Pretending you're happy costs less than admitting you're not."

I looked at the floor. I wondered if this was what all friends did—lecture you on how you've screwed up your life.

"So your life is perfect?" I asked her.

"Of course not. I could use more money, but I wouldn't trade my freedom for any contract Ackerman has ever issued."

"Everybody's free," I said. "You can do anything at all, so long as you—"

"...pay for it. Yes, I've heard. But money doesn't buy freedom, Charlie. Freedom is a right."

"That's not what the Bible says."

"Ahh, yes, Zino's Bible. The only book in the world that you can bet, the more someone quotes it, the less likely they are to have read it. Most CEOs don't even bother with it."

"It's the bible of capitalism, of course they read it."

"No, they think it's silly. It has too many rules," she said.

"Rules? There are no rules, that's the point!"

"Oh, Zino's Bible is full of rules. Rules like honesty, integrity, pride in one's work. Zino thought these qualities were paramount to capitalism. She argued that lying never worked and that cheaters were always caught. I wish that were true, but as a foundation for a system of governing? Christ, that's insane. Like Marx before her, Zino had a great theory that hinged on completely unrealistic, even idealistic, assumptions. Capitalists are people, no more or less trustworthy than socialists. People choose the path of least resistance, and for most people that includes cutting corners.

"No, most CEOs don't read the Bible. But they do love to quote it. It convinces the masses to cede all power over to corporations, and that any failure is simply their own fault. It argues well—seductively—for the virtual elimination of government and any sort of regulation of power. People cling to the 'free hand of the market' as a perfect god. They're so eager for a solution that can be neatly applied to every situation that they're desperate to overlook its faults. Those born to HighCon—children of affluent families—think that they built that wealth themselves, and that their claim on the privileges and protections of fortune are stronger than those who work under the yolk of poverty—simply by virtue of their birth..

"The wealthy say that hard work should be rewarded. But they gloss-over the fact that most poor people work far harder than they do.

"Try to get a HighCon, a man who purports to believe that competition builds character, and that giving unfair advantages is a Moral Hazard, to send his kids to a LowCon school. Ask him to start his child on a level field with everyone else and compete from there, and you'll hear a different tune."

"Yeah, but governments were inefficient, bureaucratic nightmares. That's why they called them leviathans."

"That's not why, Charlie. And you act as if you've never worked a day in a corporation. How many bosses do you have? How many supervisors? How many memos do you get? If you need to requisition something, how long does it take? How many litigators does Ackerman have? How many rules does the Ackerman Employees' Blue Book have?"

"Corporations eliminated crime," I answered

"There aren't any laws! They didn't eliminate crime; they simply defined it out of existence. It's been capitalized, that's all. Under a republic, police didn't create crime, firemen didn't watch buildings burn, and people weren't allowed to die simply because they couldn't pay for healthcare.

"Ackerman can pay for health screenings at airports, but it would cost them money. They don't, so tuberculosis gets in from Europa and it spreads. Ackerman can then make money treating the sick, and whatever paycheck you got last week goes straight back to them—you work for free now. Corporations try as hard as they can to make you think that they care about you, while simultaneously trying to rob you blind. Insurers are incentivized to cut corners and drop policies, firemen to burn down buildings, and cops to create crime."

"So your system is perfect?" I asked.

"No system is perfect. If finding fault with a system is all it takes to throw it out, you're in for a world of disappointment. I don't need perfect, but I can ask for better. A lot of the time competition is best. I like fast cars, tasty cornflakes and soft toilet paper. Capitalism makes those things possible. But we all have needs common to the human condition. We need air, medical services, and insurance—not against our own failings, but acts of God that can strike anyone. We need police, and some form of guaranteed legal recourse against people who violate contracts or hurt people. We need education and a skilled workforce. And what blows my mind is that even HighCons would benefit from these things! If a poor man gets drunk and drives, that's fine so long as he pays for whatever damage he does. But if he puts a family of five in the hospital, or God forbid kills them, how's he going to compensate for that? Just how many times can you reclamate him?"

"That's why a leviathan is better?"

"Government, Charlie, not a leviathan. A republic. They gave the mass of people a say, a means to be represented, an unbiased third party to protect people with enforceable laws."

"You mean corral them, herd them and regulate them."

"Yeah, Charlie, because you're completely free now. Life is a grand old tart!"

"But people took advantage of the system."

"Of course they did! That's what people do. That's what people have done from the dawn of man. That's why power needs to be distributed evenly, why the poor must have a voice, and why people need to be engaged."

The rain was still coming down. I had never had an argument like this before. It was exhilarating. She was a seditionist, a pagan—a worshiper of gods long dead. I had been so busy fighting her that I hadn't realized how much I was enjoying it.

"If they were so good, why did they fail? Corporatism beat out government fair and square."

"Another of Zino's assumptions that isn't even close to true. Even in the corporate world, the best product doesn't always win. Ackerman has horrible brake pads, but the firm is so big that they can leverage every competitor out of the market. General Automotive was one of the best car manufacturers in history; Panther Inc. made worse cars—at a higher price! But they had better Perception Management. Don't lie to my face and tell me that the best product always wins—I'm not even sure it wins half the time. Three quarters of Ackerman's budget goes to Marketing, Perception Management, and Litigators—and that's not including Retention. Tell me how any of those departments make products better? How that's efficient? If a corporation put its money into nothing but making a better product, they'd get wiped out.

"Once we lost the ability to moderate competition, it stopped working. Nobody makes real products, they make consumers. Darwin is a messiah, and if I don't say that I believe he's *always* one hundred percent right, I'm a blasphemer and a socialist who's afraid of honest competition. We've lost the ability to believe in any power but unadulterated self-interest. Communism may breed laziness, but capitalism breeds greed. And it's killing us."

"And what does corporatism breed?" I asked.

"Paranoia."

She had already proven herself worth far more than I was going to have to pay for her. She might have been insane, but I'd have paid ten times the hourly rate.

We argued for hours. I threw everything at her, championing the joys of corporate life and the natural simplicity of free markets. Her answers all refused to disappoint.

"Tell a man he'll get food for free, and he won't buy any. Tell him he'll be insured against unemployment, and he won't work."

"How do you figure that? I'm not saying you give away steaks and apple pie. We can make protein bars. They taste awful but you can live off them. We could feed the world Charlie—not animals or livestock—but flesh and blood people who are starving. Nobody says 'Well, I'd rather starve to death than work.' And if working gives you a chance to buy better food, get that video game you've always wanted, or take a girl out on a date, you'll do it. Why do capitalists always espouse the value of an honest day's work but assume that given the chance, nobody would ever do one?"

"So you would run a capitalist economy solely on electives? You can't make any revenue that way," I said.

"Less than ten percent of Ackerman's revenue comes from essentials. The rest is from people competing with each other for prestige and comfort. You want to get a man to buy a new car, let him see his neighbor driving one. People are never satisfied: they will always want better pools, homes, cars, boats—everything. Capitalism does that so well; it flourishes in so many places. What blows my mind is that it's always the capitalists who have no faith in the ability of the system to succeed on electives alone. Saying that we should capitalize everything is avarice. Everything, even capitalism, has a point where its use is excessive. The pigs are walking, Charlie."

I had never in my life met such an extraordinary a woman. I loved it. And I loved her.

"Oh dear lord," I exclaimed. "It's nearly five a.m."

"Oh, I'm so sorry. I didn't realize the time. You'll be billed a small fortune for this!"

"No, don't be silly, I'm the one who's sorry. You've got another job."

"I do. But I'm really glad I stayed. I guess most people would have thrown me out after the first five minutes. I had fun tonight, Charlie."

It was the first time someone had ever said that. Well, it was the first time I believed it, anyway. And it was the most incredible feeling I had ever felt.

7

I overslept, and when I finally got out the door I couldn't help but stop on the bridge along my route. I gazed at the soot-covered trees, the hazy sky and the dirty river, and found hope—not because I believed in republics, but because there was someone else who did.

When I finally got to work I found forty or so memos on my desk, most of them from half a dozen supervisors, each expressing varying levels of concern about the fact that I hadn't filed a report in over fourteen hours.

At lunch, Bernard prattled on as he always did.

"Did you ever wonder why a Delta is lower than a Gamma, even though the letter D comes first in the alphabet? It's from the Greeks. Their alphabet was Alpha, Beta, Gamma… and, well you know the rest. Honestly, the Greeks are dead and buried. People just use that archaic alphabet to seem smart. You could have an A-Con, B-Con, C-Con and so forth. Or use colors: red, green, blue…. maybe metals like copper, gold and platinum. This Greek business is so unnecessary. They meddle in our contracts, our language, even in our poker…"

Having failed to garner any attention, he spoke louder. "The business suit is outdated, too. Who still believes that you can tell the quality of a colleague by his suit? A suit tells you nothing! I waste time just putting it on. Between keeping it clean and in repair—heck, even getting in and out of it— the time I waste is like throwing money out the window. I should be able to come to work in my underwear if I want. The work is all that matters! The work!"

Corbett snickered.

"I know my mugging came at an inconvenient time," continued Bernard. "But this bill is ludicrous. They added a surcharge for it being an after-hours call. It'll take me a month to pay this off. I swear, next time I'm just going to hand my money over to the robber and be done with it."

Corbett couldn't restrain himself anymore. "The police saved your life, and you're upset over some little surcharge? You can afford it."

"They brought in an entire SWAT team. Against two hoodlums with a bat? Nobody was going to kill me. And after-hours? That's when muggings occur! How can that be a separate charge?" he said, stuffing his face with an apple fritter.

"Christ, Bernard, all you do is complain. The cost of air is up half a point, the humidity is too oppressive, Greeks are meddling with our alphabet, the cops charged you too much for saving your life… Give it up!

"Everything that goes on here is above your head," continued Corbett. "The Greek, the suit, corporate jargon, customs and traditions—it's a dialect. I can spot an Epsilon— even in an Alpha's suit—a mile away, because he doesn't wear it right. He's stilted and uncomfortable. A man who has taken the time to know which fork to use and when, who can use the right language, who knows when to be polite and when to be rude—that man communicates precision. You know who you're talking to," he said, staring at the fat man nearly bursting through his clothes. "Your suit tells me more than your ledger ever could. But yeah, I guess the way you eat, I'd complain if I had to clean that suit too!"

"Bull! It's dominance, pure and simple. I'll bet you Takashi tears off his suit the first chance he gets, dances around in his briefs!"

Corbett shook his head. "If you took all the time you spent complaining and actually spent it working, you'd make so much you wouldn't have to worry about it. Honestly, you're the laziest man I know."

"I'm two ranks higher than you, last I looked!"

"Well, we're the same grade, Bernard. And you're, what, ten years older? I'll be on the ninth floor in sixteen months, and you know it. And you know what else? At least I don't steal reports."

"Who's stealing reports?" Bernard asked.

"You!"

"I don't steal anything!" he said, shocked. "I work hard; I'm one of the hardest workers here! Of all the jealous, petty, inhuman things to say."

"You're a thief!"

"Go on, say it again! I'll sue you for libel. I have witnesses!"

I sipped my coffee. He wouldn't be filing any lawsuits. This was just part of the negotiation. Five caps here or there, maybe a game of poker, and the matter would be settled. Millions of caps a week changing hands, tamping down corporate flare-ups... an unending flotsam of cash trading hands.

"You think like a LowCon!" Corbett said. "You have no idea how anything works!"

"Oh, like you're some expert on low-contract colleagues or how they work."

"I am! I have this small community I've been investing in," Corbett continued, "right along the Capital City wall.

Nobody wants to invest there, 'cuz twenty percent of the people don't pay their electric bill. You've got to constantly get on them if you want your money. But I solved that problem. I wrote up a flyer letting them all know who hadn't paid. If I don't get one hundred percent payment from everybody, I'm cutting them off—all of them! They'll be so screwed. They should just bring back horses and carriages, lamps, frigging kerosene lamps! I'm not going to take this. They've got alternatives, and I've got quotas to make. You think Leoben isn't treating his sectors the same? If they don't like this corp, they should move. Did I tell you about Grandma Millie? She's a moocher, called me up and said she needs electricity because her grandson is on some electric heart pump. I said 'Perfect, now you have a real incentive to make sure your neighbors pay.' Honestly, the audacity to think *her* son is *my* problem. But that's the deal with these LowCons, always trying to pawn responsibility off on someone else. There's a reason they're low-contract; it's a mind-set, this 'oh, poor me' garbage. Sound familiar?"

"They're not all like that," I mumbled.

"Of course they are. That's the definition of a LowCon," snapped Corbett.

"I met one," I said.

"A LowCon? Who hasn't?"

"No, no. Someone who believes in leviathans."

"That thing from the Jewish Bible?" Bernard asked. "A whale or something? They're all dead, aren't they?"

"No, you ton of lard, he means government! He met a citizen. God, you really *don't* know anything," said Corbett. "I would love, just for a day, to have the sense of denial these people have about the world, to pretend that you can care about other people and the world will be just great. Forget actually getting anything done, building something, keeping people safe.... Name one leviathan that ever worked—ever! You can't! And yet in the face of overwhelming, insurmountable proof, you still find these people. How wonderful it must be to have the ability to completely believe in something no matter how utterly nonsensical it is. Let's all believe in unicorns and fairies while we're at it—that's productive."

Much to my relief, the conversation drifted on to other subjects.

I came home to a wife in the mood for a fight. Most of her things were loaded up. She granted me a few minutes of indignant silence. Then she began ranting that I was the cause of all her failures, that the only mistake she had ever made was to marry me, her life a cascade of ruin after that. The final proof of my ineptitude, she said, was that I had, after so many years, failed to see what an opportunity I'd had being married to her.

I marveled at her wrath.

Then she broke down crying, apologizing for overreacting, telling me she was sorry and saying that we needed to work out our problems.

She's behaving like a citizen, I thought, *acting as if we share more than a marriage contract.*

It was partly my fault. I had told her I'd be a high-ranked Gamma someday, maybe even a Beta. I played the part I needed to land her, that of a real go-getter—regaled her with plans and schemes for advancement, building sub-corps or branch divisions, revolutionizing corporate markets. I had honestly thought that I'd wanted those things. But I didn't, and that had proven itself out. And marrying her? That was pride. She was beautiful, argumentative, ambitious and unattainable. I enjoyed the prestige of being married to her far more than the actual practice of it.

If there was a way to fix this marriage, I didn't want any part of it.

She grabbed all of her things, some of mine, and left. Moments later my ledger buzzed to let me know that she had cashed out. She was gone forever.

* * *

"That man over there," said Linus, pointing to a poster of a large man in a suit and hat, "is Al Capone. Everyone knows he was a great capitalist. What most people don't remember is how jealous the leviathan was of his success. He profited by selling alcohol and prostitution, services *the people* wanted. But the dammed leviathans said they knew better. They outlawed what he was doing, and when he had to use violence to defend himself, they called him a gangster and threw him in jail. If what he had been doing was wrong, he'd have had no customers, and he'd have been out of business—pure and simple. No matter how much money he made, all they did was vilify him. My god, the dark ages."

I nodded casually. The café was bustling, but I didn't really notice.

"To your new life," he toasted. "Beatrice was dead weight. It's marvelous you got rid of her—even got her to think it was her idea, let her take the hit on the divorce. Good man!"

I sipped my coffee and smiled as graciously as I could.

"You know, you seem different now. More self-confident," the Beta observed.

I laughed. No, I had no confidence. In fact, I had come more and more to realize that everything I had ever believed in was wrong. I regarded the system now, not a force of God or nature, but as just that—a system. I knew less than I ever had before.

"You know what this means, don't you?" Linus asked, pleased with himself.

I shook my head.

"We need to play."

When I realized he meant poker, I had to hold back a chortle. Poker, this game that gave me nightmares, panic attacks and cold sweats.

Oh my god it was just a game, a pastime. Just because Linus thought it was the ultimate expression of life didn't make it so. Winning or losing at poker meant nothing more than winning or losing at poker. I was who I was, and would be just as much after the match as before it. How on earth had I ever let six little dice become one of the greatest sources of anxiety in my life?

I put a single cap to my chest. I didn't bother looking at the serial number—I wouldn't have known the odds anyway. Linus let out a bemused chuckle.

He bid, and I countered. He paused, not out of any genuine hesitation, but to remind me that he was still in command; to remind me that no matter how much I had changed, no matter how much courage I had, his victory was inevitable. He gave his second bet, and I called. We flipped the caps over and read them together.

I lost.

I gave him the cap. It was the easiest and fastest game I had ever played, and as close to having fun playing as I was ever going to get.

He stirred his coffee, eying me suspiciously, yet grinning with pride.

"Is there a problem?" I asked.

"No, not at all."

Despite his denial, Linus still kept a Mona Lisa smile. I wasn't in a rush—I wasn't the one who had a job worth hundreds of caps an hour waiting for me at work. So I waited him out.

"You know," he said, "it may not have occurred to you, colleague, but that was the most remarkable game we've ever played."

"Nah, I wasn't even close to winning."

"Of course not. What's remarkable is that in all the years we've played, this is the first time you ever called me."

"That can't be right," I said.

"I assure you, it is. Until today I could've used fictions numbers that don't even exist, and you wouldn't call me. You only play defense, Charles. It's why you've been a born loser, up until just now. Beatrice was far worse for you than I thought. This is the first time we've actually played. Well done."

This was extremely serious. I had thought that I could hide my new nature, that I had lived in the system long enough that I could continue to blend in. But I couldn't.

I *had* changed. Irreparably. And in a way far more pronounced than I had thought. And it would only grow more obvious.

There were a host of other problems too. I couldn't stomach managing perception anymore—not for Ackerman, not for anyone. I could stick to the basics, report innocuous mistakes like spelling errors or factual inconsistencies, but I wouldn't be able to make a living on that for very long. And it was only a question of time before somebody suspected something. Heck, Retention could already be on me. Linus, Corbett, or even Bernard—they could all be undercover agents. Even if they weren't, there wasn't a single one of them who wouldn't turn me in if they thought they could profit from it.

There was a clock on me now. If I didn't do something, the question wasn't whether I'd get myself into trouble, but when.

"I'm proud of you, Charles. You're ready to be a Gamma now. It's going to happen for you, I have no doubt. You've evolved; you've reached the next stage. Congratulations."

If there was anything I was sure of, it was that I was never going to be a Gamma.

8

I had found Kate, but I still didn't know what had become of Sarah Aisling. I'd need money, but that was very hard to come by in large quantities. The economy ran better if colleagues spent money instead of saving it, so savings accounts were prohibitively expensive. Only the wealthiest could afford them. I had an escrow account, but buying out Beatrice's share of the apartment put that in the red.

About all I could do was secure a large loan (at a high rate of interest). It didn't matter; I had no intention of paying it back.

I called a cab and went to the library. Though they didn't advertise the fact, the truth was that the Galt Intercorporate Library was one of the most profitable corps in history. They offered two things no other library did. First, in addition to carrying practically every legitimate text ever written, they also had an extensive catalogue of pornographic, perverse, and subversive literature.

Second, they didn't monitor their clients or report their activity to any other corp… anywhere. That level of anonymity was worth almost any price, and the library knew it.

At any given time there were about a half dozen corps trying to shut them down, get them to restrict usage, or to monitor their customers. Negotiations on these issues almost always ended in violence, so the Galt maintained a small but effective military force.

Perimeter bollards and Jersey Barriers surrounded the entire building. Behind those was a twelve-foot chain fence, with razor wire and machine gun nests. The only gate had more security than the Atlas train station. It was UltraSec, if such a word existed. Scanners, chemical detectors, and bomb-sniffing dogs all stood between the outside world and the library. The building itself was a huge concrete structure with a three-foot-thick steel blast door.

Despite all of this security, they prided themselves on expediency. From the line it took only ten minutes to get inside.

I soon found myself standing in front of real books, ancient tomes from corporations and governments alike, computers with faster access to data than I had ever dreamed. The heretical works of John Stewart Mill, John Locke, and Thomas Hobbes could all be found in their own, original words.

An open terminal gave me access to Sarah Aisling's records, more material than I could possibly go through. Her market value was pennies, and her status was listed as "detained." The case had been escalated less than a day after my report, and they transferred her to the Citadel. I'd never be able to scrape together enough to learn her fate there.

But Kate was Sarah's friend, and might know what happened, maybe even know of a way to help. I looked up Katherine Wolfe in every personnel directory I could, but I couldn't find her. She had been filling in, and since she didn't work for Ackerman—or the rental agency for that matter—I had no idea where to even begin looking for her.

That left me with the Arab woman.

I found a list of the rental company's employees. One by one I pulled their work licenses and found an Arab woman with dark skin and curly black hair named Jazelle. I hadn't gotten a good look at her, but she looked like the right one. Her contact information was the same as the agency's, so I just printed her license.

I rushed home and, rummaging through my old boxes, managed to find my very first Ackerman ledger, an old Epsilon piece of junk. I was supposed to have turned it in when I got a Delta contract, but kept it for sentimental reasons. It was deactivated, and even if it weren't, the firmware probably couldn't even log into CentNet. But it might survive a cursory examination. I put on the dirtiest, dingiest clothes—moth-eaten and stale—that I could find.

I had never been in LowSec before, but I knew the stories: rape, murder, and even cannibalism. It was all Epsilons and NullCons. The police couldn't make any real money cleaning up crime, so stations were few and far between. Only a few broken-down fences and barbed wire, between LowSec and NullSec, kept out the barbarians in the wild.

I took a cab to Capital City's western gate. I hadn't traveled that way in years. You could actually see the gradient, watch the city dissolve. Houses became duplexes, condos became apartments, lawns became patches of dirt, and windows became smashed shards with bars over them. By the time I reached the fourteen-foot wall encircling the city, homes were missing entire walls, rooms and roofs—all held together by rope, plastic bags, and rotting wooden beams.

The city wall looked like hell. The beige paint had chipped off and there were scorch marks from detonated mines all along its length. Still the razor wire was mostly intact, and the wall did its job. Sniper towers, spider mines and

Bouncing Betties were ready to cut down anybody stupid enough to try to go over the thing.

"So many people," said the driver, "trying to get in here. They want our jobs, our money. Forget earning a living, they want to break in and steal one."

The rate was a flat thirty caps to get into Capital City—enough to keep out the riff-raff. You could get out for free—they didn't even check your credentials. Still I saw a line in both directions.

"Who the hell is trying to get out?" I said, as we slowed and pulled in behind the car in front of us.

"Day-workers, mostly. Low and NullCons. They don't have a contract, so they're slave labor. Karitzu protections don't apply. Some of them get—what, maybe thirty-five caps a day."

"But it costs thirty just to get in here."

"Yep. They get five—take home."

It's their own fault? They just need to work harder?

"Slaves?"

"Sex trade, mostly. You want to have sex with a twelve-year-old boy, it's hard to do if he's got a contract. Well, it'll cost you a lot anyway. But null contracts, they're starving to death out here. Fifty caps will buy you the right to do anything you want to anybody."

"How many people are out here?"

"Eh…" he said, waving his hand.

As we approached the gate, I saw a small car coming the other way. The guards stopped it, and the driver began arguing with the officers. One of them came around to the back, pulled out a revolver, and shot the trunk open. A man burst out and made a dash for the city line. The agent calmly raised his pistol and took aim. A shot rang out, then another and another. The man fell to the ground. Meanwhile three other agents had pulled the motorist out of the car and begun beating him.

The driver looked at me through the rearview. "Don't worry," he said. "This happens all the time. At least a few times a week. It's not dangerous, they're careful not to hit anyone of value."

"Are they going to kill him?"

"Nahh... They'll come close, and then send him back as a warning. Won't do any good."

We crossed through the checkpoint and into LowSec.

The place looked a lot like I had imagined, like the pictures I had seen on television: decrepit stone, brick, and wooden buildings; dirt, filth and debris strewn everywhere. Nothing I had seen, though, did justice to the smell: mildew, rotting cabbage, fetid milk and raw sewage. Broken windows were covered with garbage bags, and water trickled from all sorts of places—broken downspouts, clogged gutters, and hydrants. There probably wasn't a fire company within fifty miles; the buildings weren't even worth a day's pay.

"Let me out a few blocks from the address."

"Sure... Don't want the wife to know you're coming down here, eh?"

"Something like that."

I got out of the cab, and the driver sped off. Not until then, unshielded by the four corners of the car, did I really understand that I was in LowSec.

I looked both ways down the street, but I didn't see anybody. LowSec was supposed to have a huge population, but it was empty. Maybe, I thought, the place was so huge that some areas were deserted while others were social and economic hubs. Maybe the driver just dropped me off at an inauspicious spot.

I hadn't gone more than a few steps before I stepped in excrement, my first conclusive proof of life. I walked over to a rusted lamppost, leaned against it, and tried futily to wipe it off.

Two blocks down I heard panting. Down a small alleyway was what looked like a wire fox terrier standing beside a dumpster. The dog's coat had once been pretty, fluffy and white. But now it was muddied and patchy with mange. He was missing most of his teeth, and one infected eye was swollen shut. Despite all of this, he tilted his head and wagged his tail when he saw me.

Then I noticed the boy hiding behind the dumpster. He was ratty and skinny, his clothes an earthen brown and his face muddy. The dog returned his attention to the lad, who was smiling and holding out a piece of flesh. He licked the child's hand, and the boy knelt beside him. His tail started flying around, and he licked the boy's face wildly as he nuzzled the creature close.

Suddenly he slipped a noose over the dog's head. As it struggled, a band of children came out from an open doorway and grabbed the animal. It was emaciated, but had enough meat on it to feed them for a night. The boy slung the mostly dead dog over his shoulder, and they darted into an abandoned building.

I looked back down the long street. The sun would be setting soon. I wondered if I was close enough to a radio tower for my ledger to work, maybe call a cab. The agency was supposed to be only a few more blocks down, but I couldn't see any offices or businesses around.

I continued down the street, and noticed more children following me. They were hard to see—never really coming out from behind buildings and stoops, creeping back into the shadows whenever I turned to look. But they were there. Despite all my efforts to blend in, they had known from the moment I arrived that I didn't belong. Maybe it was the cab, a LowCon company, but still from inside the City. Or maybe it was my shoe—why would anybody out there even bother wiping it? I worried that they were considering how plump I was, and how long I could feed them for.

I'd been hearing noises for some time, but it wasn't till then that I began paying attention to them. They had started with what sounded like whispering, or the rustling of trash in the wind. But these kids had, no doubt, told their friends, brothers, sisters and parents about the spoiled brat MidCon bumbling his way through their neighborhood. I noticed tapping too—banging coming from pipes and lampposts—a coded signal echoing for blocks. Without electricity or phones, still everyone within two miles knew I was there. As I approached each new block I could see the odd person or two glaring out at me.

Where they had earlier taken some pains to hide themselves, now they didn't seem as discreet. It worried me. I picked up the pace, but still couldn't find the agency. It hadn't even crossed my mind till then that the address could easily have been fake.

I was about to dart into the nearest building when I caught a glimpse of the agency's black and yellow rental sign under a crust of grime and benzene-soot.

It was a converted Laundromat. Inside, baked into the walls, were the silhouettes of nearly two dozen washers and dryers. An emphysemic old man sat far in the back, playing solitaire, drinking a urine-colored liquid from an old olive oil bottle, and coughing up phlegm. The fan nailed to the ceiling had no blade-guards, and it oscillated with a horrific grinding noise.

A man sat with his feet up on a long desk, which ran lengthwise down the room. He was bald, with hawk-like eyes and a thin nose. He saw me, but if he could tell that I didn't belong, he didn't show it. He casually got up and flicked his terminal on.

"It takes a minute to warm up. Can I help you?"

"Yes, I rented a friend, Kate. My name is Charles Thatcher."

"Oh yeah, the overages. Long night. She didn't screw up anything, did she?"

"Oh—no," I answered. "In fact, I wanted to speak with her for a few minutes if I could."

"Well, she's not due in today, and we're not scheduling her at the moment."

"I see. Do you have a number where I could reach her?"

"I'm sorry. I'm sure you understand we can't give out friends' numbers to clients. I can have her contact you."

I shook my head. "You're outside my Karitzu. My corp might find out if you called me. I'll just try again next week. When might be good?"

"Like I said, we're not scheduling her right now. I can offer you a different friend, if you'd like."

I shook my head. "No, don't worry about it. Maybe I can try again later, or go with another firm. Do you think you could call me a cab?"

The man nodded. When I stepped out onto the curb, I saw no trace of the curious neighbors or children.

A few minutes later a cab arrived. I climbed in, and the driver asked me where I wanted to go.

"Do you have an anonymizer?" I asked.

He looked me over, suspiciously. "Sure. It's eighty percent more."

"Does it work?"

"The bill will say you hired a trade consultant—all on the up and up. You can even put it on your ledger."

"Do it. Head a mile east, as if you're going to the city. Then stop." I commanded, handing my ledger forward.

"Pay when we get there."

"Run it. It's going to be a long tab."

The driver beamed when he ran the ledger, still laden with borrowed cash.

I sat back into the dirty, beaten old seats. For a moment I felt the pride of ownership, a pride I had purchased. In MidSec I was an average guy. Here I had complete authority over the driver, enough money to sell and buy him a hundred times over. I wondered if HighCons felt like that all the time.

"Got a romantic interest? Don't want the corp to know?" the driver ribbed.

"When we get there," I said, "come back to the spot you picked me up, but on the intersecting street, kitty corner to the building. I want to be able to see who goes in and out of there."

"You got it."

He didn't say anything else. If there was one thing money bought well, it was silence. I burrowed into the back seat and waited.

"Mr. Thatcher?"

I had fallen asleep. It was night, and about half of the street lamps were out. But by the dim light of the rental sign, I could see a young olive-skinned woman approaching the office.

"That her?"

I nodded. She went inside.

"What if she goes out the back?" I asked.

"Nah, she'll come out the front where there's more light."

A few minutes later she came back out and began heading down the street. I reached for the door handle.

"Hold on!" cried the driver, reaching for the dome light. "You open the door, she'll see us! You know, if she gets into a car, how you gonna follow her?"

I hadn't thought that far ahead.

"Stay in here, we can watch her from the car."

"Are you kidding?" I said. "She's gonna notice a car following her."

"Nah, I can do it. If I switch to the battery, this thing'll be dead quiet. If we stay between the lampposts, stay a couple hundred yards back, she'll never see us."

Every person I added to this intrigue increased the chance that I was going to get caught. Still, he seemed to know what he was doing (which was more than a little unsettling in its own right). I offered him a bonus of two hundred caps if he got me to her house without her knowing.

"Yes sir!"

So we followed her. Every time she approached a light, he'd release the brake, rolling forward into another dark spot between the lamps. I felt like a stalker, like I was committing a violation. It didn't seem to bother the driver any.

Half an hour we did this. She would turn down a street or vanish between buildings, and more than once I thought we'd lost her. The weather was getting worse; the moon vanished behind the clouds, and it was already beginning to drizzle. But my driver never failed to find her again. As she went deeper and deeper into LowSec, fewer and fewer homes were lit.

Finally she turned into an industrial park. It began to rain heavily, and I could no longer make her out. He pointed to a large warehouse with a very dull firelight shining through the windows.

"She went in there."

"What is this place?"

"Everett Park. It's a communal."

"You mean like communism?"

The driver shrugged. "Don't know. It's just a place where a bunch of people take over a building. If there's an owner, they may pay him something to look the other way. Maybe not."

I authorized his bonus.

"Pleasure, my man," he said. "Listen, bro, this can be a rough neighborhood. I can stick around if you'd like. I mean the nearest working phone could be miles away."

"I'll be fine."

The warehouse was about three stories tall. If it was a shelter, I couldn't imagine it being a good one. Windows were smashed out, the fire escape was barely hanging on, and there were large cracks in the wall.

As I got out the smell of sulfur hit me. I made a mad dash for the side door, which opened onto a stairwell. The air was so thick with smoke, I thought I had stumbled into a building fire. But I could smell tobacco, wood and paper pulp, and looking out over the main floor I could see nearly two dozen fires in everything from oil barrels to metal pails. Already the lack of oxygen was making me dizzy

Even with a thirty-foot ceiling and half the windows open, how are they not suffocating?

It was a shantytown. Wire frame bunks, old prison mattresses, shopping carts and makeshift partitions were scattered everywhere. The air was rank with the smell of rotting meat, body-odor and feces. Water dripped from the roof and broken windows, and everything seemed damp and moldy.

I couldn't make out any faces, so finding Jazelle would be nearly impossible. I made my way as best I could, looking for someone who looked like her. After a few minutes I had covered only a small part of the warehouse, but somehow managed to work myself into a dead-end corner behind several drums and a large wooden industrial spool.

"You lost?"

Through watery eyes and thick smoke I could make out three men approaching me. The first was a large bald man with a boxer's nose and meaty hands, callused with scars and rope burns. The second was thinner, but carried a bat and had a vicious look on his face, while the third walked with a limp, dragging a metal pipe behind him.

"I... Yes, I'm looking for a friend," I said.

"You ain't got any friends here, HighCon."

"No, no, I'm a MidCon; I've got a Delta contract. My name is Thatcher, I'm looking for Jazelle."

"Jazelle ain't got no HighCon friends."

"No, I'm a Delta contract—almost a LowCon myself! I met her at work."

"*Almost* a LowCon, eh? Think you'se better than us?"

"The last thing I want is trouble. I just need to talk to Jazelle."

"Seems to me if you'se her friend you w'udn't be following her."

"I'm not following her."

"Yes, you is. Come out of that cop car."

"Oh my god, that wasn't a cop car, it was a cab."

"So you *was* following her?"

"Yes, but not like—"

A fist met my jaw, and I tumbled back onto the concrete floor. I took a few staggered breaths before managing to get up on my hands and knees. The pipe hit me in the chest, and I felt a sickening crack. I tried to ask, to beg, them to stop. But I couldn't even tell if I was breathing. I fell to the floor, and they grabbed me by the legs and began dragging me over the concrete. It was chipped and cracked, and I dug my nails into every crevice I could find, clawing at it. They hauled me over debris, bits of broken glass and metal digging into my chest and stomach. They flipped me over, and I looked up just in time to see a boot coming down on my face.

9

I woke up against a steel drum, my legs sprawled out on the floor. It was hard to breathe. My nose was running, so I wiped it on the back of my hand, but instead of mucus, I came up with blood. My hair was wet and matted from a gash in my head, and my knuckles and fingertips were raw and bleeding. I wiggled my toes—they hurt, but they moved. I couldn't move my right leg, though. Whether it was suffering from the old injury or from the beating I couldn't tell. But splayed out like that I kept sliding down, so I grabbed my leg and propped it underneath myself to try to get more comfortable.

I was in a corner somewhere. Someone had opened a nearby window to let in a little fresh air, but at least one of my ribs was cracked, so it was hard to breathe anyway. Around me were several four-foot bookshelves, a dingy mattress, and a small metal pail hosting a fire. Book spines— the pages torn and used for insulation or kindling—littered the floor.

"Who are you?" Jazelle asked.

She sat in an old wooden chair, watching me.

"My name is Thatcher."

"Don't lie."

"I'm not lying. My name is Charles Thatcher."

"What are you doing here?"

"I came to find Katherine."

"I don't know any Katherine."

"You know, Kate. You dropped her off at my apartment. I rented her for the night."

"There is nobody named Kate who works at our agency."

"She was filling in."

"Our agency doesn't send unlicensed friends into Capital City. It would violate our contract with Ackerman and half a dozen other firms."

I scooched higher up the drum.

"I'm not trying to blackmail you."

"That's all your type ever tries to do. I didn't drop anybody off at your place. I've certainly never met you."

"Please. My name is Charles, but she called me Charlie. I rented her. I don't want any money; I just want to talk to her."

"Charlie? The MidCon? Ackerman Perception?"

I nodded.

"What the hell are you doing here? Did you want a refund?"

"I told you, I want to see Kate."

"She said that all you two did was argue."

"Yeah," I grinned. "So she remembered me too?"

"Don't flatter yourself. She wasn't *that* impressed. Why do you want to see her so bad?"

"Well, to be honest, when I decided to come, I hadn't actually priced baseball bats into the equation."

"What do you want to see her for?" she repeated.

"It's private."

"Well, since I'm the only one who knows where she is…"

"I wanted to know more about the republic."

"My god," she said, rolling her eyes. "She wasn't going on about that, was she? Oh, Mr. Thatcher, I'm so sorry she got you so worked up. You know, that is just like her. She's new to the friend business. I told her to make stuff up to make herself more exotic, to engage you, give you guys more to talk about. She is supposed to be getting you excited, to enjoy the friendship. I'm so sorry if you misunderstood, or if she crossed a line. Most clients know that friends are faking. Was she your first friend?" she said, handing me a towel and some water. "Oh, this is a disaster. I feel so guilty. I wonder if we have any pain killers around here."

She examined the wound on my chest. "Oh, Spag did a number on you, didn't he?"

"Which one was Spag?"

"The big one."

"She wasn't faking," I said.

Jazelle nodded. "She was. I'm sorry. Her job was to chat you up. She has talent, but her choice of subject matter... I'll make it up to you. We can get you a credit, send you a professional next time. Staff came up short and we sent her out. This really is all my fault, I recommended her to the boss. I hope you won't take it out on the company; we have lots of good, reliable friends. She just acted unprofessionally."

I dabbed the wounds on my face and shook my head. "If you believe that, then you don't know her half as well as you think you do."

"I'm one of her good friends, I know her just fine, and I'm telling you, there's been a huge mistake. Listen, I can get you your money back—even a bit more for your trouble. And your medical bills, of course! We'll take care of this."

I gawked at her. "Oh, my god. It's not just her, it's all of you—the entire agency."

"Okay, now you're just trying to extort us. How much are you really looking for?"

"Is everyone down here like this?"

"Christ, you higher contracts. All Epsilons and Zetas must be citizen communists, why else would they be poor, is that it? They're lazy, useless…."

"No, you're not lazy. You believe. You're actually looking to change the system—not just for your own sake—for everyone. You're a real citizen."

"If you're just going to sit here and insult me—"

I laughed. "Don't try to manage my perception. I've been doing it a lot longer than you have. You're a citizen."

I heard an uneasy rustling in the shadows, just out of view.

"Do you know what could happen, you coming down here?"

"Well," I said, dabbing my nose, "I might get a fine, maybe lose a rank or two. Worst case I could pay it off in about six months."

"Christ, you arrogant ass, I mean to us. They won't be polite, they won't fine us, and there won't be any charges or indictments. They'll come in here with Tommy guns. They'll go floor to floor, spraying automatic gunfire everywhere. Armor-piercing rounds, they'll cut through ten people like tissue paper—through walls, hitting people in other buildings. It won't matter how many people here are 'guilty.' They'll mow down children and newborns. They'll kill everyone; they'll call it an uprising. They'll reclamate our bodies and get a nice bonus out of it. That's what they'll do, Thatcher."

My first instinct was to protest, to defend Ackerman. I was going to tell her that they were a good firm, that whatever they did was in everyone's best interest. I had said it so many times, managed so many perceptions, that I thought that way by rote.

But it wasn't true.

Like a person, the corporation only did what was in its own interest, only without the burden of consequences or conscience. Somehow I had gone my entire life knowing corporations were ruthless, soulless paper constructs. I had said as much a thousand times. But no matter how often I had said it, somehow I never actually recognized it.

I had found a den of citizens. But I didn't care, either as an economic opportunity or for the novelty of it. I didn't care who Jazelle was.

"I just want to see Kate. Please, just once."

"You could be an agent, Thatcher. You can't prove you're not, and we can't take the risk."

"No," I said. "I can't prove it. But I've already seen you, this place. It's not as if I don't know who she is. Let me talk to her. I'm talking to you right now. What's the difference? I just...."

Jazelle stiffened. I shouldn't have tried to sneak in. I should have just waited, or just rented Jazelle myself. My own impatience was going to get me killed.

"You know," I said, "it's just as possible you're setting *me* up. I've taken a risk coming here too. I just want to talk to her."

For all she knew I was a lovesick client. Heck, for all I knew she was right.

"Corporatism breads paranoia," I said.

She took in a deep breath and then nodded.

"All right. You'll be blindfolded. We'll let her make the call."

10

They threw me into the trunk of a car, and drove me around. I can't imagine a trunk being comfortable even under the best of circumstances, but bruised and bloodied, joints stiffening up, it was dreadful.

Believing in government wasn't technically a crime. Neither was failing to make a profit. Heck, neither was being a citizen. You can't commit a crime without a contract. But it wasn't until I had lain there, waiting for them to let me out, that I knew they had every right to be worried.

They drove for at least a half hour before I was dragged from the trunk, up a stoop, down a hallway and into an apartment. They sat me down and, after hearing a few whispers, everyone appeared to leave.

"Hello?"

A hand grabbed my hood and pulled it off. It was Kate.

My lips were swollen, joints and muscles all stiff, and I had bruises and welts all over my body. Still I couldn't help but smile with, what I must imagine, was the goofiest grin anybody has ever seen.

"Oh, Charlie, my god."

"Hi Kate."

"What did they do to you?"

"Nothing," I said, with the smile of a newborn who first recognizes his parents.

"What on Earth were you thinking? Why did you want to see me so badly?"

"Well, like I told Jazelle, I didn't really think it was going to be this hard. And I thought colleagues were paranoid."

"It's corporations we're afraid of. Tell me, is there a single colleague you don't fear?"

The apartment was not bad for LowCon. The walls were painted cinderblocks. The table also rested on cinderblocks. The windows were cracked, but they weren't missing any panes. Pipes ran down the length of the walls, all patched and expertly wrapped in plumbing tape. She even had a television, though it heavily favored the green range of the spectrum. The place had a quiet dignity to it.

She handed me two painkillers and a cup. I tasted the water; it was fresh.

She has a solar still.

"I'm sorry. They're really worried. I'm not licensed. You could be the police, or even Retention."

"What would Retention want with you? You're not even Ackerman."

"I was filling in for a friend who was arrested a week ago for stealing water. It's not a huge deal, but it was Ackerman's water. Now she's gone, and nobody knows where she is or why. If Retention took her, they could make her say anything. It won't matter what the truth is. They'll perceive whatever gives them the most profit in perceiving. If they're looking for more thieves—or worse—they'll start by sending scouts. Someone like…"

"Was she a good friend?"

Kate nodded. "She was my best friend."

My chest tightened. It had been an incredibly bad idea to come.

"I just wanted to talk to you," I said. "You know me, I'm not a spy. I was just so happy to have met you."

"I met you after the arrest. You could be anybody."

"I'm a Delta from Perception."

"Maybe. It's sweet that you wanted to see me, Charlie, but what are you doing here?"

I wished I could tell her that I had thought that far ahead.

"I guess I just wanted to know more about government."

"Government? Couldn't you have just gone to the Galt? They have everything you could want to know about it. Coming out here, at this hour, it's insane."

"You're right. I'm afraid of every colleague I know, everybody. Except for you. You're different. I guess I wanted more of that," I said, looking at my shoes. "There's nothing at the Galt. You know it, you've lived it."

"I'm not a real citizen, Charlie. I've never actually *lived* in a country or republic. Honestly, what do you need to know so badly?"

I didn't know. I had lied to her—even with the baseball bats and the beating, I'd still have come. And I had no idea why.

"I guess I wanted to know if they were... were they happy?"

"Oh my god," she said. She slumped into a chair. "Oh my god, Charlie."

"Were they happy?"

"Do you know what could happen to you if you get caught?"

"I don't care. Just tell me, were they happy?"

"I don't know, Charlie. I think they were, but people can adapt to just about anything. Some people are happy in corps and others sad under governments. No matter how good things are, people will find things to complain about; they always do."

"But you must know if they were happy."

She sighed. "Compared to people now, yeah, I think they were happy. Republics caused problems, too, but for the most part they were an impartial third party that protected people. They had laws—rules nobody could break no matter how much money you had, and a system to enforce those laws. And people did cheat the system, but enough power was left to the public that you couldn't leverage the whole thing. At least that was the theory of it all."

"I have a mentor, his name is Linus. He says people broke laws all the time, hardly ever got caught or brought to justice."

"Sometimes it happened. Like I said, no system is perfect. If that's what you're looking for, good luck, I've never seen anything that makes me think a perfect system exists."

"How can you know that they were happier?"

"Well, I'm not sure how to define happiness. But if I had to, I'd say it's the variety of things you can do, and the amount of time you have to do them. A prisoner may have all the time in the world, but nothing to do with it. A colleague might be able to afford almost anything, but spend all his time acquiring and defending his wealth."

"But competition is natural. It's a universal constant: stars compete for hydrogen, planets for carbon, and solar systems for space. All resources are limited. Isn't competition the fairest way to distribute it?"

Kate smiled. She stood and walked over to the stove. "When was the last time you ate something?"

I shrugged. She took out a small petroleum burner and lit it. "We haven't had gas in this building for about twenty years. It's slow, but this works."

"You cook food?"

She nodded.

"Isn't it safer to…?" I stopped myself. She couldn't afford anything processed or sterilized. I wondered if they killed their own food out here. I thought about the terrier.

"My father taught me how to cook. It's good to know how to, and it really is a lot of fun. Takes a lot of skill to do it right."

I had never thought of cooking as a matter of skill. It was, as far as I had heard, little more than putting slabs of meat onto a hot surface.

"Cook something too long," she went on, "and it becomes tough and hard to eat—the flavor and nutrients are all gone. But not enough and you can poison someone. And there's a lot you can do to make something taste really good. I grow onions out back. An hour on low heat with a little lard, and they caramelize—they'll make anything taste great. Timing is important too. If you throw something on too early or too late, you'll ruin the whole thing."

She pulled out an iron skillet and put a dab of tallow onto it.

"Love, true love," she said, "is cooking on a cast iron skillet."

"Oh?"

"Sure. They're hard as hell to clean, and they're heavy, so nobody uses them. But to this day nobody's invented a better cooking surface. They hold heat perfectly; distribute it evenly. My father always said that the number one ingredient in food is love. I thought he was just being cute, but it's true. Love is a cast iron skillet."

I watched the tallow start to soften.

"They're good, too, for whacking Ackerman agents that come through the door."

I went to the window. I hardly needed to pull back the curtains—they were so thin I could see through them. The alleyway behind her house was barely wide enough for two people to walk shoulder to shoulder, and trash was piled so high that the bins were buried under mountains of it.

"So where are your parents?"

"My mother," she said, dicing up a few potatoes, "died of cancer. Dad raised us, my sister and me."

"So you learned about the government from him?

Kate didn't say anything, and for a moment I thought she hadn't heard me.

"He was a library clerk," she continued. "He'd bring us books when he could. The rare stuff, the republic stuff. These were books from actual countries, philosophers and writers talking about economics and government. He used to read to us by candle-light every night."

Her voice trailed off. She was tossing a thin meat of dubious origin onto the skillet, trying to hide the fact that she was crying.

"You loved him, didn't you?"

She shook her head. "No, I didn't."

She tossed the mixture, then put it back onto the flames.

"I wish to God I did. But I hated him. I thought he was weak. He'd read those books, and all I could think was that he was using them to excuse his own failings, to justify why he was nothing more than a clerk. He worked ninety-hour weeks, and I thought he was lazy. Can you imagine that? Every argument he read about the superiority of a republic made me hate him more. Brooke, my older sister, ate it up. We'd fight all the time; I called her a communist, looter, plunderer, lazy, disloyal… I hated her even more."

"What happened to them?"

"The corp got her. She hadn't done anything, but they said she violated the 'interests' clause of her contract. Who gets to decide that? Christ, the term is so ambiguous, come to work ten minutes late and technically you're violating it.

"Anyway, there was so much money against her that the judge went the company's way. She was tried and convicted. Dad sold everything we had to get her out, but it wasn't enough. They took it all anyway and then tried him on bribery charges. Brooke was reclamated. And Dad," she said, "he was sold to a medical company for his organs."

I grimaced at the tallow in the pan.

"Oh, God no," she said. "We don't buy lard or soap on the open market. A friend of mine makes it from deer and squirrel suet."

Still, I didn't think I could eat it. I looked back out into the mud-brick alleyway.

"Did you ever find out who turned your sister in?" I asked. She didn't hear me.

"Anyway, that was it. I was done. I left and came here. I made a life as best I could. I hunt deer and cook, and that gets me by. I have some of my dad's old books; my friends and I share and talk about the republic. We go into NullSec every now and then, to hunt or to try to find old libraries or records."

"You go into null security areas?"

She nodded. "A few times a year."

"Aren't they a wasteland? With cannibals and stuff?"

"Yep. There are roaming tribes of people; they'll eat anything they can—even you. There's about a billion bodies out there too, if you believe the history books. Most of the city is buried under thirty feet or so of ice."

"The city? You mean New York?"

She nodded.

"It's real?"

"Yeah, it's a couple of days north of here. You can get there a little faster on a snow-sail. NullSec isn't pretty, but we have a few weapons, and we know where we're going most of the time. I actually like going. I imagine it's what archeology used to be like, going into Egyptian tombs, fighting booby traps and old mummy curses. I see something new every time I go."

I was scared at the very thought. But I wanted to go, too. I breathed deep. She saw me and laughed.

"Did you know that the moon is white?"

"Get out!"

"Nope. I've seen pictures, records. It's the sulfur that makes it yellow."

She knew everything.

"You really came out here to see me?"

I nodded.

"Of course competition is natural, Charlie," she sighed, "stars, planets and all that. Sure, it exists, in some way, in all systems. But to assume that it's all there is—that's simplistic. Entropy exists in all systems too. Does that make entropy all there is? Cooperation exists in all systems, too, even stars and planets. All these things exist everywhere; there's no 'universal constant' that describes everything.

"You see what you want to see. The truth is that the glass is both half-empty and half full. What you can control is how you choose to see it. If I give a beggar a quarter, you could say I was altruistic, because I helped him. But it's just as true to say I was selfish, that I gave him that quarter to alleviate my own sense of guilt. Neither view has a monopoly on the truth of it. People never do anything just for one reason.

"But what's funny is that this charge of 'unnatural' behavior comes from the capitalists who believe the most in dominating nature. Pasteurization, immunization, antibiotics, air conditioning, toothpaste—these are all direct assaults on nature. The people who most enjoy conveniences of modern living—as far from natural forces as possible—will be the first to tell you that to ask them to spend a dime to help others is to spit in God's face. Giving litigators to people who can't afford it is immoral—as if being the victim of a crime means you deserve to be victimized. They say giving medical treatment to people who can't afford it is unfair, as if there's any fairness in who gets cancer. It's unjust to give people free schooling, as if there's any justice in who is or is not born into a family that can afford an education. Fairness is nothing more than the distribution of wealth and power as those who already have it see fit. Money lets you buy favorable interpretations of right and wrong, and that benefit accrues quickly."

She shook her head. Then she cleaned a knife and chopped up some kind of green plant before tossing it into the skillet. Finally she opened a small cabinet and pulled out a yellowed jar.

"This is poteen."

"Is that liquor?" I asked.

"Yeah, but not like whisky. It's a disinfectant. Don't drink it, you'll go blind," she said, grabbing a towel and gently applying it to my wounds.

The lights flickered and went out.

"Did you pay your bill?" I asked.

She laughed. I could hear her walk across the room to a small makeshift fireplace. She pulled out a rod of Firesteel, which she struck, igniting a small pile of kindling. From that small fire she lit several candles and began distributing them throughout the room.

"The power is always going out around here. We only have electricity about half the time."

"What about heat?"

She shrugged. "The fireplace works, when you can find something to burn. I have blankets. You can wear a couple of layers of clothes at a time, too. In a pinch you can even huddle around the candles. It's rare that people actually freeze to death out here."

With what I made in a week, I could have redecorated the whole place: put in real curtains, fix the windows, and get a working television. But I knew she'd never take the money. Apparently even citizens had pride, just like everyone else.

"Do all LowCons think like this?" I asked

"I wish. Three quarters of all colleagues in the world are Delta-grade or lower, less than one percent are Alphas. If all low-contracts thought like this, we wouldn't be having this discussion. But a lot of LowCons are just trying to keep their heads above water. Others have been oppressed for so long that even hoping for relief is painful. And some of them love Ackerman more than most executives do."

"How's that possible?"

The potatoes and a little cabbage were next to go into the skillet. Gradually, agonizingly, the heat began to overcome the iron, and the hash began to sizzle and pop.

"There are a million reasons. Beggars can't be choosers—so, naturally, they want to be. They want dignity, and there's dignity in choice. If you're poor and espouse the merits of social services, people say 'Well, of course you do, it's in your interest.' But vocal support of a system that is stacked against you grants a sense of pride, of autonomy. And if you think that there's nothing you can do about it anyway, this sense of pride doesn't cost you anything.

"Besides, probably ninety percent of LowCons would bet their lives that they'll be that one half of one percent who actually gets out of here, becomes a HighCon. Who wants to rock that boat, or tempt fate by arguing against the system?

"Then there are the people so desperate to scrounge something up for themselves that they prop the system up, because it's better to be a living doormat for the higher contracts than a reclamated hero for the lower ones.

"And heck, let's not forget those people who are just what HighCons think they are—lazy uninterested bums.

"There are so many reasons why LowCons put up with it that people just choose whichever one suits them best, makes them feel better about themselves. They decide that that's the whole truth and stereotype the whole class."

The bleeding had stopped, and whatever she had given me for the pain was taking effect. The swelling had gone down. As my eyes had adjusted to the darkness I took the opportunity to look around a bit more. The apartment had a similar layout to mine, but smaller. The appliances were left unplugged in case of power spikes, and bars guarded the windows. The bedroom was tiny, consumed mostly by a twin bed; an old mattress on it with the life and comfort beaten out of it.

I already felt more at home than in my own place.

"So we can't do anything?" I asked. "Nobody wants to fight, nobody wants to change things? This is just the way things are?"

Kate smiled. "Of course not. They can't get inside your head, Charlie. They can't make you be anything you don't want to be. You can't control them, but you can control yourself. And you know that. I know you do, because you chose to come here. They don't own everything."

Maybe not there, they didn't. But that was only because they didn't care about LowSec. It had no gas, power was intermittent, and the water was probably poisonous. Their lack of material wealth meant safety. It meant freedom.

I was breathing again, and my ribs didn't hurt anymore. But the anesthetic had made me dizzy. I wasn't going anywhere that night.

"We aren't stars, Charlie. People wish we were. It's gratifying to be mean, to visit injustices—done unto you—onto other people. Vengeance is cathartic, and to distill everything down to raw competition is a great excuse to justify it without having to worry about the effects of your actions on others.

"But they're hypocrites, all of them. I see people espouse the benefits of corporatism all the time, and all I can think is, *why are they telling me this*? The ruthless executive who convinces people he has a heart of gold succeeds far better than the one who goes around telling others that they should be ruthless too! Why increase your competition? It's ego, that's what feeds colleagues. They have complete contempt for everyone, and an overwhelming desire to be worshiped for it. The truth? These capitalists don't want to get away with murder; they want you to *choose* to let them get away with it.

"Ask these same people, Alphas and advocates of competition as a moral system—those who say that competition creates strength, and that giving things away for free, or insulating people from their failures, creates weakness—ask them to let their loved ones live without the added benefits and protections of wealth behind them—and nobody will cry foul faster. Hypocrisy never troubles a true capitalist.

"Take Takashi. One of his sons is in oil—all he's ever managed to do is drill a lot of dry holes into the ground. He's bankrupted three different companies. Does this corporate magnet let his son suffer the consequences of his mistakes? Nope. He bails him out. When the poor screw up, it is their own fault; when the rich do, it's someone else's. You can let the poor suffer their mistakes, but never kin."

She scooped the mash onto a couple of plates and handed me one along with a beaten up fork. "I don't have knives, sorry."

"I wouldn't have it any other way."

I couldn't identify the meat on the plate. But it was crisp on the outside, soft inside, and very tasty. And she was right about the onions. She broke out some alcohol, something we could drink. With the meds it made me light-headed and happy. I never wanted to leave. I didn't need my mid-level contract anymore, or my MidCon apartment or my MidCon job. Just her.

She saw it before I had even moved towards her. I threw my arms around her and kissed her as if she were the first woman I had ever met. By any measure I knew, she was. I kissed her as though we were the only human beings alive, as though the universe itself existed only inside that tiny apartment. She was love, life, all of the things I had never known. She was the antithesis of everything I had been taught. And at that moment love was something stronger and more passionate than I had ever imagined.

11

When I was six, I caught one of my teachers having sex in the school bathroom. I told my parents, who sold their silence to her for several thousand caps. Years later my mom sold me to Ackerman. My first real girlfriend hacked my work account, stole my reports, and was promoted for it.

I couldn't even trust my own wife.

I lay in Kate's arms, naked, on her trampled mattress. I'm sure I was a terrible sight with gashes and scabs on my face. But she ran her fingers through my hair like it didn't matter. No money was to be had, no profit in any measurable sense. But I was happy.

She could have been Retention, the entire rental office nothing more than a front to catch wayward colleagues. And I could just as easily have been one too, come to ferret out pockets of resistance to corporate theology. There was no way to know, so we just accepted what we had.

No doubt Kate had other suitors, men of her world—LowCon born and educated—who were predisposed to principles of cooperation. Common sense said that's where her heart should lie. But those men hadn't ever been on the other side. It was one thing to rail against things you could probably never get anyway. But I came from MidSec. I had lived in Capital City. I knew the alternatives. Like Sarah Aisling, I was there by choice.

As we lay in bed, she found the scar running down the length of my right leg. She ran the tips of her fingers down it. I recoiled.

"I don't mind," she said.

I wanted to be perfect for her, no scars or disfigurements. She just nuzzled me closer.

"What happened?"

The room was dark, too dark for me to feel comfortable telling the story. I reached for my pills before remembering that I had thrown them out.

"It's okay; you don't have to tell—"

"I was up at Allenhurst, on an interview for a job in one of the maintenance buildings. Nothing fancy, I wasn't skilled, and only an Epsilon at the time. I'm at the front desk waiting with maybe a dozen or so other applicants, and an Alpha comes in. His terminal is on the fritz, he's put in a bunch of petitions to get it fixed, and he's sick of it. He wants to know why he can't get anybody on the phone.

"Well, the methane generator had sprung a leak. I'm passing him to go to the interview, and it blows. The whole building comes down on everyone.

"I wake up, I can't feel my leg—honestly, I thought I must have been dead. I couldn't see or hear anything. After a few minutes I recognize the sound of dripping water—some burst pipe somewhere—and I realize that I'm alive, my leg crushed under a beam. Then I hear digging.

"Well, I can't figure out why they're bothering with any of us. Then I realize that the Alpha is buried right underneath me. He's worth a hell of a lot, so they triangulated his ledger and started digging like crazy. But they can't get to him without cutting out the beam, and when they do, I get out."

I took a deep breath.

"Besides the Alpha, nobody else in the lobby was worth rescuing. I guess if you're going to get blown up, doing it next to an Alpha is the way to go."

She rubbed my leg once more, and put her head on my chest.

As the days passed, I spent more and more time in LowSec. When someone asked where I was going, I ignored them. They assumed that I *was* going to LowSec, rebounding from my divorce with thrills both perverse and cheap. I always used the underground, paid cash, and never took my ledger with me.

While Kate trusted me, her friends were another matter. She had a clique of them, like Jazelle, Spag and the other two who beat me, the bald man at the rental office and a few more. None of them liked me, and they made no effort to hide it. They would come by at odd hours of the night, whispering quietly between them. Her apartment turned out to be just a block from the warehouse. They'd hold meetings, which would end abruptly when I arrived. I never asked about these machinations, and she never volunteered. She had gotten them to agree to let me see her, and that was enough.

She began teaching me to survive, how to spot dangers and keep from being seen, how to collect and distill rainwater and how to trap and skin rabbits. She even began teaching me how to cook.

My job became unbearable. I couldn't work for Ackerman anymore, much less in Perception. My colleagues did nothing but squabble, preen, and gripe, and I wondered how I had ever tolerated it.

"People used to live to be eighty—like, average people." Bernard would say.

"That's a lie," said Corbett

"It's true. Study history."

"Any society where the average person can live that long has real problems. If it is true, no wonder they collapsed."

"It's true!"

"You just want me to spend five caps looking up something that doesn't mean anything anyway."

"It's true."

"Go to hell, socialist."

"Because I know history I'm a socialist?"

"No, it's just one of the reasons. You're a weak commie bastard, and I look forward to watching you get your ass handed to you."

That was the routine, day in and day out. I worked tiny, nuisance reports, nothing more vicious than typos and the occasional dangling modifier. At night I'd make my way into LowSec, browse the shops and pick up a little lavender oil or paper tablecloths. It was all there once you knew where to look. Sometimes we'd move the dining table aside and just eat on the floor. We talked about citizens, and about governments and republics, or about ancient literature, culture, and history. Sometimes we just talked about the weather. We talked about colleagues like Corbett and Linus, friends like Jazelle and Sarah, and the family neither of us had seen in ages. She'd crank up the turntable and I'd listen to songs that I imagined hadn't been heard in a hundred years. She showed me around LowSec, showed me old buildings, bombed-out aquifers—even a transmitter which she said had once broadcast television for free. She took me to an old flood-control channel. A sign over it read "World's Oldest Ditch (500 years)." I wondered by what right they could claim to know that, and found myself fighting the urge to find some small, obscure place to fill it in a bit.

And there were solar stills everywhere, thousands of them. They were hidden under tiers, behind tarps or on back porches. Everybody had at least one, and most people had four or five. A funnel would capture rainwater and dump it into a plastic-wrapped bucket or can. The sun would evaporate the water, which would condense and collect on the plastic and eventually drip down into another bucket as clean, drinkable water.

"So everybody's taking water?"

"Yep, right out of the air. You have to, no water comes into most of these buildings, and the sewer systems are four hundred years old. They used a split pipe back then, water on one side and sewage on the other. You'd get sick if you drank it."

"If everybody's doing it, why was Sarah the only one to get arrested?"

"That's a good question. We hide the stills and we're usually not worth the bother anyway. I don't know who turned her in. Maybe someone didn't like her, or a neighbor needed a few caps to keep from starving. I don't know."

I was an outsider in both worlds. Finding Kate had put me in considerable debt with Ackerman, and I wasn't doing my job in any meaningful way anymore. Like Eric Forestall in cubicle 721, I had creditors I'd have to stay ahead of. But I couldn't simply vanish into LowSec; I needed Kate's help. But her friends hadn't come close to accepting me. And why should they? For all they knew, I was an agent, and even if I wasn't, Ackerman would come looking for me.

Then, one night, the light in cubicle 721 went out.

12

A number of colleagues had gathered in the cantina, though Bernard was not among them. Corbett sat drinking coffee and going over his day's literature.

"Quiet today," I said.

"Yeah. Well, any day Bernard isn't here is a quiet one."

"Where is he?"

"I don't know. Trying to find a new kid to mentor or something. How that fat man gets anyone to pay for his time is beyond me," Corbett said. He picked up his coffee mug and gave it a sour look. "You know," he said, "with all this Kabul business, you'd think that coffee would be better—at least until they get rid of the ragheads."

"Add some chicory," I said. "It'll add flavor. Heck you can make coffee out of chicory if you need to."

"Chicory? What the hell?"

"It's a plant."

"I know what it is. Why the...? How do you know you can put it in coffee?"

"I... well, I've been learning to cook," I answered. "It's actually fun, and you have a lot more choices if you cook for yourself. It's fresher than anything you'd get in here, that's for sure."

"Oh my god, Charles! It's bad enough you ride that deathtrap into work every day. Now you're learning to cook? Do you know how that looks? You do realize that you're supposed to go *up* in rank?"

"Cooking is not some LowCon thing; anyone can do it."

"It's LowCon. Face it, they're the only ones who can't afford processed food."

"Alphas have private chefs. They eat the real thing."

"Yeah, and the chefs are all LowCons, I guarantee it."

"You always say that knowledge is power," I told him. "So why not learn everything you can? Like how to cook?"

"I'm not going to cook. You're just pissed that someone suckered you into learning crap like this and now you're trying to get me into it. It won't work."

"It's fun," I said. "Cooking actually takes skill—"

"Whatever," he answered.

Weeks passed, and I hadn't received a payout for my Aisling report. It was a bad sign. I was starting to suspect that Sarah Aisling had actually been a person of consequence to Kate and her friends. I became sadder and sadder, keeping this secret from Kate. She was getting sadder too, and I wondered if it was about Aisling.

One night we sat in Kate's apartment, talking about my new favorite subject, the republic. The power was out again, it was raining, and the building shook with nearby strikes of thunder. The windows all leaked and puddles formed on the floor.

"You know," she said, "man has walked the earth for sixteen million years. But only in the last two million did we develop language. We can choose what we see, Charlie. People say Darwin believed in competition. But he believed in evolution too. Compassion exists, and Darwin himself would say that was proof that we benefited from it. The corporatists will tell you that compassion is like a vestigial tail. Why is it such a leap to think it might be an evolution, like language, something that allows us to do more together than we ever could apart? It's been proven, mathematically, that trust is essential to success. But corporations don't breed trust, they kill it."

She's talking about trust. Does she know something?

"How do you *prove* trust is good?"

"A mathematician named Nash did it. Before him people said that the best outcome occurs when everyone works in their own best interest. But he showed that self-interest was only half of the equation. The best outcome actually comes from people thinking of themselves and the group equally."

This is a message. She knows. She's testing me.

"Say two crooks are working together. They commit a major crime that carries five years in prison. But the police can only prove a smaller crime that carries two years. So they separate the men and offer each a deal—rat your partner out, and we'll drop the lesser charges on you.

"Now, if one of them takes the offer, he goes free, while the other gets seven years—two for the lesser charge and five for the greater one. But both guys know this. So what do they do? They each rat other out. So now each gets the lesser charges dropped for cooperating, but gets five years on the testimony of the other.

"Now, capitalists will point to this and say 'See, each of these men did the best they could for themselves. Each knows the other will rat him out, so they cut a deal to get five years instead of seven, which is an improvement.'

"But here's the thing; if they both kept their mouths shut, they'd only get two years. It's not freedom, but it's a lot better than five. The reason they talk is because they're in competition. They're each so busy trying to protect themselves from the other guy that they damage each other. Competing for the best possible outcome, no time in jail, prevented the worst outcome of seven years, but it also prevented the better outcome of two years. If they had both agreed to shoot for the two years, they would have gotten it. If they could trust each other, they'd be a lot better off.

"And this kind of situation isn't rare—in fact it's the norm."

"But that can never work," I said. "How could you trust the other person? I mean, if he rats you out, he goes free? How can he resist that temptation?"

How can you trust me?

"That's the rub. The men must both trust and be trustworthy. It requires long-term thinking, something corporations de-incentivize and are notoriously bad at."

"But all it takes is one person gaming the system," I said. "If even one person betrays that trust... How can it ever be sustained? You'll never get everyone to be trustworthy."

"Well, yeah, that's the problem. If one person breaks the trust and goes free, others see that betrayal is rewarded. So they begin doing it too. Soon everyone will betray everyone, and greed becomes a virtue. Then everyone is back to getting five years, shouting 'Thank God we betray each other, or we'd be getting seven.' And then the worst option is to trust your colleague, because you'll be taken advantage of.

"In Zino's Bible, every capitalist implicitly trusted every other capitalist. They were simply good people. And if that was always the case, capitalism would work exactly as Zino predicted—a perfect libertarian utopia. But it's not. Without a strong third party to regulate, destruction and short-term thinking are rewarded; entire generations live at the expense of their grandchildren, and Zino is turned on her head. You need a system of laws and an entity capable of enforcing those laws—common rights and guarantees, regardless of wealth or power."

"The leviathan…" I said quietly.

"No, Charlie, government. Your colleagues call it the Leviathan, the great whale from the Jewish Bible. But that's not where we get the name from. *Leviathan* was the name of a book written by Thomas Hobbes. He defined the 'social contract,' saying that without sacrificing *some* freedom for the common good, life was 'cold, nasty, brutish and short.'"

"That's not communism?"

"God no. Even Nash said that the best actions were the ones that *equally* balanced the needs of others with the needs of the self, balanced selflessness and greed. Greed is exactly half of Nash's equation. The criminal isn't expected to sacrifice himself for his cohort and say, 'I confess to the crime, I'll take the seven years so my partner goes free.'

"What a good government does, what a republic does, is moderate competition; allow the tug of war, but never let one side walk away with the rope. They also establish rule of law, and a safety net below which people cannot fall. Everybody can vote, everybody can share power, no matter how rich or poor. Everybody has rights, and the republic is strong enough to enforce those rights. Police, health, mail, education, the things that everybody needs are guaranteed. Corporations can compete, but they are kept reasonably honest and not allowed to over leverage and risk people other than themselves. People will abuse the system, some corps will get away with crime, but the distribution of a minimum amount of power and resources to all people hedges the damage. And it forces the wealthy, not to be slaves to the poor, but to have a modicum of concern for them, because they can vote."

"Do you trust me?" I asked. I was glad the lights were off.

"Of course."

I wished she had said no.

"This is about my friends, isn't it?" she asked.

"Well…."

"You hardly ever see them. They're always sneaking around, calling and slipping me papers, coming by at night.

They don't trust you. I know that. You can't blame them. I know you're not Retention or Acquisitions, but I have to respect their concerns. You arrived just after Sarah was caught. Earning their trust will take some time. And she was a person of some importance around here."

"Importance?"

"Well, she was our—well—leader, for lack of a better word."

Dear god. I crafted a perception of Sarah as the head of a seditionist organization just to make a quick buck. But I was right.

"Do you know what ever happened to her?"

"No. Her 'crime' probably wouldn't have been a big deal, but she's stubborn and not all that pragmatic. We were willing to chip in for an advocate. She said no. I thought she meant she could afford one, but instead she just stood there and told off the judge. I don't know why she thought that was a good idea. He actually didn't seem to be too bothered by it, but her case was escalated anyway. We haven't heard anything. Maybe they somehow thought they could get more money from her. We don't even know if she's alive."

"Why would she fight with the judge?" I asked.

"There was a hotel fire. The building had revolving doors, and when the fire broke out, people panicked. Too many tried to get through at once and the door couldn't turn. Six hundred people burned alive.

"Now back in the days of the republic, there were regulations that said when you had revolving doors you also had to have emergency doors that opened out. There were millions of little regulations like that, and the republic could shut down places that didn't comply. *Of course* those rules made life harder on business, installing extra doors, inspections, higher heating bills. But this hotel went bankrupt, six hundred people died, who does that help? And nobody going into that building knew it was a death trap. You can't inspect every building you walk into yourself.

"Sure, in the days of a horse and buggy, you didn't need specialized knowledge to make sure that you were getting a good product. But in modern times how are you going to make sure there's no cadmium in your paint, or that there isn't lead in your water, or that the building you're walking into is safe? Regulation isn't pretty, but…."

"She's that way because a hotel burned down?"

"No. She was in that fire. Her whole family was. She made it out. They didn't.

"I think she misses her sister the most. Talks about her all the time. Anyway, that's it. She's a bit of a fanatic when it comes to the republic. And not that I don't agree with her, but going to jail for the rest of your life doesn't help the cause. Nobody on earth will ever know that she stood up to that judge."

I know.

"What do you think they'll do to her?"

"Whatever will make them the most money."

"Why don't we try to get her records? If we all chip in—"

"Oh, Charlie, you're so sweet. But how are we going to do that? We start poking into those records, someone's going to ask why. They'll start investigating, and then we'll be next. Besides, I'm not sure you have that kind of money."

"If she's gone for too long, what does that mean?" I asked.

"Reclamation," said Kate, gravely. "Of course. But you need to do a lot more than steal a little water or tick-off a judge for something like that."

"But she's gone missing, right? You should have heard something by now?"

"Yeah. I mean we're worried, sure. Why are you so bothered by this?"

I almost fell out of my chair with nausea. She put her arm around me, but I threw it off and held my head in my hands.

The man who had escalated Sarah's report was long since dead. I didn't know him anymore; I was ashamed that I ever had. It was another lifetime, a distant memory. But it dragged on me like an anchor tearing through my life. It wasn't Charlie who had filed that report, it was Thatcher, a man I'm not sure I ever understood, and someone I didn't like.

If I could have undone it, I would have. I'd go back to my old life, back to that dark cubicle, writing reports and listening to Corbett and Bernard bicker. I'd even go back to my marriage, if it meant that I had never written that report.

Certainly Kate and her friends—all of them—would've been better off.

I want to be reclamated. Leave me to rot at Ackerman.

She looked at me, worried. But she loved me only because she didn't know what I had done.

"I turned her in," I said finally.

"What? What do you mean you? You didn't even know her."

"No... Not for stealing the water. Her case. It came into Perception. It was a small matter, nobody cared. I thought if I wrote it up, told people she was a citizen, that I could make..." a fortune. That was the word I was looking for, a fortune.

"How did you know she was?"

"I didn't! I thought I was making it up."

I could see in her mind the tumblers falling into place. I hadn't picked her agency by chance.

That blasted clipping. How could such a thin piece of tissue paper cause so much destruction to so many people? I've as good as reclamated Sarah myself.

I wanted to leave, but it was too dignified. I couldn't deny her throwing me out.

"I'm sorry," I said. Apologizing seemed so useless. But what else could I do?

You're a failed colleague, and an even worse friend.

She fell to her knees and began to sob. I found myself hoping that her friends would show up—maybe Spag—and see what I had done. They'd make me suffer proper. But I couldn't bear her crying. Overcome by cowardice, I ran out of the apartment. I didn't even stop to close the door, just fled down the hallway, over the stoop, and out into the darkness.

Acid. Maybe the acid is bad tonight and I can let it eat me away.

The rain was clean. I cursed my luck. The one time I wanted rain strong enough to eat flesh, and I was denied by nature herself.

I ran down the street, into an alleyway, down another street, and around the nearest corner. I didn't watch out for glass or nails in the road, pedestrians or the occasional car, I just ran. I caught a broken lamppost, and felt a gash open on my arm. It didn't hurt enough, so I looked for another injury I could inflict on myself.

In my blindness I fell down a small gully into a drainage ditch. I knew immediately where I was—the abandoned school a few blocks from her apartment; the five hundred-year-old ditch. I wanted to get lost where I could never be found, and I had failed at that too.

Mud and refuse washed over me.

This will infect my cuts for sure.

I felt a shoe come off and wash away. I lay a minute before slowly climbing up the bank and back onto the main road. I was shivering, and I realized I'd freeze to death long before any infection spread.

Lightning struck, and I saw a person across the intersection from me. Nobody but lunatics and madmen had any business being out there in that weather.

Kate came up to me, and in one fell swoop drew her arm back and slapped me hard, very hard, across the face. I had no resolve left.

Good. Again. Harder.

I prayed she had a knife, something she could stick into my belly, twist and pull up—let me die in a garbage pile in LowSec. It was still a better death than most people out there got, starving to death, though not nearly as bad as I deserved. She wouldn't do it. I don't know how I knew that—she certainly could kill me if she wanted—she had the nerve, had the skill. But she wouldn't. So I eagerly awaited the next slap.

It didn't come.

"Why?" she shouted.

What the hell? That's what she wants to know? How could she not know? She knew what it was to be a colleague.

The truth? People always tell you that hard work leads to success. But it's hardly ever true. Prestige, power, and influence are the only real currencies. People use those to buy the *favors* they need to make money. The people who make the most money come from money, have the most to leverage and can sit back and let their money do the work. You want to know who's going to make the most money? Just look at who was born into it. The single best indicator of where you end up in life is where you start, no matter what the capitalists tell you.

I did it because I wanted into that club.

Sarah had been nothing more than a name on a piece of paper. I hadn't seen her curly blond hair, her bouncy demeanor or fanatical dedication to a cause she was willing to die for. She had no parents, children, friends or even colleagues—she wasn't somebody's child. She was just a name.

"Why?"

"I... I thought that if I could—"

"Why did you tell me?"

I stammered. From the moment I met her, I knew that I'd have to face this sooner or later. How could she not know that?

I want to be punished. That's why.

"I... you had to know."

"You didn't have to. You could have just gone on pretending... pretending that you didn't know her. Why didn't you?" she said angrily.

Because I want to know what it feels like to have the only person you love in this world hate you. Then I might feel better.

I shook my head. It would have been the only sensible thing to do—pretend like it never happened. We were happy together. It's not as if anybody would ever have found out, and telling her wouldn't bring Sarah back. If I had possessed even an ounce of self-preservation I'd have buried the secret, even from myself.

"Let me go," I begged.

I had stopped wiping my eyes. The rain had matted my hair to my face, and I couldn't see her any more,

But I heard a soft voice. It simply said "no."

"Just let me go. Go home, I won't come back, I promise," I pleaded.

"No."

"End it all right here. I don't want to fight anymore. I don't have anything left."

"No," she said.

She came up to me, threw an arm around me, and led me back home.

We sat there quietly. I was disinfecting my wounds, and she was toweling off.

"I could buy her out," I said, "at the very least pay her fine."

"You don't have that kind of money. None of us do. Besides, you're already leveraged to the hilt."

"I'll find a way to raise it."

"How? I mean, if anyone could just raise that kind of money, they'd already be doing it."

"Maybe if we pool our funds, we can buy her out?"

Kate shook her head. "At what cost? There's always someone we need to bail out, someone in trouble—there's more trouble out here than we can afford. People are starving to death."

"Maybe just enough to buy her records then. I can get you some money," I said desperately. "Then at least we'll know where she is."

"Knowing where she is might make us feel better, but it won't help her at all. And if I buy the records, they'll want to know where I got the money. That'll draw attention we'd rather not have."

"I'll ask for her records then, as a follow-up to my report!"

"How many times have you ever followed up on a report in your career? Five or six? You have to have some kind of reason to follow up—they're going to ask."

"I'll say it's because I am so concerned for the company, because she's so dangerous."

"You're going to help her by reminding Ackerman how dangerous she is?"

"My god," I said, "how can you be so blasé about this?"

"Oh, my poor Charlie," she said. "I'm not. But what do you think life is like out here? People vanish all the time. Ackerman can come for anyone for any reason, and sometimes people come back, sometimes they don't. All we can do is keep our heads down, hope they don't decide we're all worth more rendered into machining lubricant."

"I have to do something."

"I don't know about you, but I want to live. And we're not going to live if we can't overcome our mistakes, move forward, and worry about keeping the people we have alive. I've got some experience with this, and I can tell you that you can spend years blaming yourself; it's cathartic, it's easy, and it's a great excuse to not go about the business of living your life. Wallowing in self-pity is as futile as working for that huge payoff at Ackerman. But you're not the only one suffering; neither is Sarah. People out here, citizens, are struggling to stay alive. If you can't forgive yourself, where will you be?"

"What would she think, you bedding the man who had her killed?"

"We don't know she's dead. We don't know that it was your report that escalated her case. We don't know who reported her in the first place or why. Heck, we don't know for sure why she was arrested—stealing water might have just been an excuse.

"We need to focus on what we have, and not what we don't. But if she knew the man you are today, what you're risking by coming here, I think she'd forgive you. I hope she would.

"And I haven't given up on the idea that maybe someday you'll be able to ask her for forgiveness yourself," she said.

"I want to do something. I want to bring down Ackerman, the whole system—corruption and greed—I want to end it."

"I know."

"There must be something we can do, some way to bring it down. I mean, if we don't do something, they'll keep picking all of you—all of us—off. This is no way to live, waiting for them to come grab us."

"I'd rather be me than them any day of the week. Every day I thank God for putting me on this side of the wall and not the other."

"I want to do *something*," I said. "I want to start being part of the solution, not part of the problem."

She nodded. "I understand. Do you trust me, Charlie?"

I looked at her. "Of course."

"Good. Then go to sleep."

13

I was sitting at the café, quietly stirring my coffee, lost in thought while Linus rambled on about lagging indicators of unemployment in the current economic climate.

He noticed, and asked if I had been listening.

"No. I'm sorry, you were talking about... What?"

"Is it Beatrice?"

"Oh no, god no," I chortled.

"Then what? There are plenty of other people who are willing to pay for my time if you're not interested."

Of course Kate's friends don't trust me. I haven't done anything. I haven't risked anything for these beliefs—stood by them, fought for them. So long as I say and do nothing, citizenship is just a belief.

"I was just... Well I'm tired, that's all."

"You gave me that excuse last week," he said.

"Well, I've been busy...."

"Do you remember the story of the boy who cried wolf? It's about a boy whose job it was to guard the village's sheep. One night he got bored, so he cried wolf, and laughed as all the villages came running. The next night he did it again, and again on the third night. On the fourth night, however, a real wolf came. He cried for help, but the villagers thought it was a trick, so none of them came, and the wolf ate him. Do you know what the moral is?"

I shook my head.

"Never tell the same lie twice. Lies have to be fresh, constantly changing. You cheat on your spouse, come up with a new excuse every time you're home late. Don't, and you get eaten.

"I don't mind you lying to me, Charles, I expect it. But for God's sake, change it up a bit. You're certainly finding something interesting, and it's not me."

"I've been thinking about... Have you ever heard of the Prisoner's Dilemma?" I asked.

"Of course, Nash's theory. I'm not a complete dolt. Is that what's bothering you?"

Whatever answer I had expected, this wasn't it.

"God, you're white as a sheet. Is everything okay?"

"I... well, I guess I wanted to know what you think of it."

"Oh, genius, of course, every word of it. It's basic economic theory; we'd be living in caves without it."

"The Prisoner's Dilemma?"

"Yes, Charles! What's wrong?"

"I guess... well, I guess I don't understand it. Could you please explain the theory to me?"

"Of course. Nash was a philosopher who discovered that people who work together do better than those who don't. In the Prisoner's Dilemma, two thieves are caught and threatened with jail time. If they work together against the police, they each get less time than if they don't."

I gulped down the last of my coffee and ordered another one.

"Charles, did you get hit in the head? Are you sure you're all right?"

"And you're okay with that?" I said. "What Nash said?"

"Of course. Aren't you?"

"But I thought Nash was a mathematician, not a philosopher? Are we talking about the same guy?"

"Of course we are. Those are just labels. Call him what you like. He *was* a mathematician. But Darwin was a biologist, and he is the father of the social fabric of society. These people changed how we look at the world. I think it's wonderful that you're learning Nash, but look at you, you look like you're about to jump out of your seat."

"But how do you reconcile cooperation with modern society?"

"What do you mean? It's the foundation of modern corporatism; that's what we do, we work together."

I became lightheaded, my heart began to flutter, and my chest tightened. The next coffee arrived, and I downed it even faster than the first.

"Jesus, you'll give yourself palpitations. That has a lot of caffeine. Listen to me, I want you to slow down!"

I wiped my mouth on my sleeve and looked around the room for relief.

"What's wrong with you? You're acting very strange. You're quite bothered by this. Is it the idea of cooperation that troubles you? Look at you; you can barely sit in your chair!"

"Nash wasn't... He didn't talk about... he was talking about common interests!"

"Oh, of course he wasn't. There's no such thing as common interests, Nash knew that."

I fell back into my chair. I could see him now, as I had seen Beatrice on the night she left. I could see Linus with the clarity he himself possessed.

I had thought that if I tried hard enough, since Linus was a bright guy, I could win him over with the strength of my convictions. But we weren't even speaking the same language. We knew the sounds, the grammar and vocabulary, but the words all had different meanings.

Linus already knew all the arguments; he had processed them all. But instead of expanding his own understanding or worldview, he simply integrated each new fact into his previously held beliefs, supported by the impenetrably circular argument that competition was superior because it had beaten cooperation in a competitive match. Those were the rose-colored spectacles through which he saw the world, the system of weights and measures he used to judge life and call it fair.

Kate never denied the need for competition. But it wasn't the entirety of all life. It was a system among many—each of which had to be applied in a constantly evolving and changing mix by people engaged in the system. That was the key—even the best of republics degenerate when trusted to the leaders alone. That complacency had killed the republic, a refusal to invest in the work of both finding and then staying on top of that mix. That same blind faith would kill the corporations just the same.

I was now, irrevocably, a citizen.

Kate had said I should keep a low profile. But I couldn't straddle the line any longer. I was Sarah Aisling, incapable of hiding my contempt for the system. I'd spent my life doing nothing, just letting the system do whatever it wanted so long as it didn't trouble me any. I kept quiet and cloaked myself in the lie that silence wasn't an endorsement.

Linus saw competition everywhere he looked, as the very fabric of nature. But he saw it that way because he chose to see it that way, to live in that world.

I'd love to have said that he'd die a lonely, miserable man because of the humanity he sacrificed. But it wouldn't have been true. Linus would die a very wealthy man, an executive, maybe even CEO. He was already happy, fully enmeshed into the system. He derived pleasure from the system, fed off the lies he told and the people he outwitted. He would die happy because in the end he believed the most important lie, the one he told himself: that he was the greatest colleague in the world. There's no bridge between you and a man who can invent an entire reality.

"Are you okay?"

I smiled and relaxed my shoulders. "Yeah, of course. You were right, too much coffee. I'm sorry, I should stop taking advantage of these prices."

"It's tough, they're at record lows. You know, you are an odd duck, Charles," Linus said, sipping his coffee. "You need to play."

"I'm not going to play." I said.

"What?"

"I'm not going to play."

"You're just off the map today. What has gotten into you? Is it your contract grade? Everyone has fears and doubts. You're just lazy, undisciplined. You need to learn to control..."

Linus' voice trailed off. He was still holding the coffee nearly to his lips, eyes fixed out the window, but the smile fell from his face.

I turned to look, and then I heard a loud crack. The café became quiet. A man in a tan trench coat had just passed the newsstand. He staggered towards us, a look of surprise on his face. Blood began seeping through his coat, and a renewed determination overcame him.

Another shot rang out. His shoulder lurched forward as he was struck, and he tumbled to the ground. Linus dropped his coffee and threw himself on top of me. As he did, the man outside exploded, wiping away the newsstand in a single stroke. A deafening wave of nails, ball bearings, and shattered glass washed over us.

I was back at Allenhurst. The building lay on me. I couldn't see or hear anything. *So this is it. This is how my life ends.* I wasn't breathing. But if that were true, how could I smell the burnt flesh and sulfur? I couldn't feel my leg; I couldn't feel anything, except water trickling down through the rubble. That was how I knew I was alive—the cool wetness of ruptured water pipes. Drifting in and out of consciousness, the math was easy—the risk to workers wasn't worth rescuing anybody. Just bring in the bulldozers the next day and begin clearing the rubble.

I wasn't at Allenhurst. I remembered, then, that I was in a café, in the middle of Capital City.

I shouldn't have come back. There's nothing left for me at Ackerman. You were silly—silly to worry about anything. Reports to your bosses, meetings with Linus, the games with your colleagues, they're all distractions. You should have married Kate, had children, watched them learn and grow, explored the ruins of NullSec and stolen water. You should have done things differently.

I realized that I was being crushed, not by a building, but by the weight of the former rugby champion. And in a flash, the weight was gone.

I sat up. The air was filled with dust, but the café was brighter than I had ever seen it. The posters were tattered, the blinds had been ripped from the windows, and the floor was littered with metal and glass. A loud, shrill siren going off somewhere in the distance. At first I thought it was an air raid warning, but it was just my own ears.

I eyed what remained of a booth—splintered and shredded, with the stuffing blasted out of it. My hand was wet. I glanced down to see that it was resting in a growing pool of blood. As the ringing subsided I could make out moaning and screaming, though it was hard to tell where it was coming from. I thought I had better check myself for injury, and half-heartedly patted myself down, though I could have had a dozen broken bones and wouldn't have noticed.

I stood up and tried to brush the glass off. Blood had matted the smaller pieces to my clothes, making them tough to wipe off. The air looked dusty, cotton bits floating in it like dandelion seeds. Bodies were slumped on the tables and on the floor. Some people were dead, others were clutching their wounds.

I looked around for someone to help me. I wasn't sure what anyone could do, or even if I needed help. Maybe I could just walk out of there. I hadn't tried walking yet. Then I became vaguely aware of my name being shouted. I tried to concentrate. Yes, it was my name. Someone was calling me.

Linus was on his knees amidst the carnage, leaning over a badly injured woman. He tore his shirt into strips and began bandaging her wounds. He grabbed a steak knife and cut the pant leg off a dead colleague and fashioned a sling. He shouted my name again. I couldn't hear what he was saying, but gathered that he wanted me to come over. He pointed to her neck, where a severed artery was already rapidly soaking through the bandages. I tentatively grabbed her throat.

"Press hard!" I heard.

I pressed harder.

"Hard, dammit!"

"I'll choke her," I protested.

"If you don't choke her, she'll bleed to death!"

Pressing down hard, I felt her larynx under the flesh of her neck. She looked up at me, gurgling as she struggled to breathe. Her eyes were alive, pleading, as if she really believed that there was something more that I could do.

"You got it. Reconstruction will be here in two minutes. Let go and she dies!" Linus jumped up and moved on to another victim.

The woman was older, maybe in her mid-fifties. She was dressed like a HighCon, but her skin was old and wrinkled—the signs of a Delta or even an Epsilon. Even as her eyes begged for life, she began clawing at me—trying to wrench me off her. I clasped my hands even more tightly around her throat.

At Allenhurst I had been on the other side. Now, at the café, I wanted to save this woman. As I clasped my hands around her throat, I begged God to let her live. Let me save this one life—not because it meant anything to Ackerman, but because it meant so much to her.

By the time the medics had arrived, she still had a pulse, but her eyes had closed. I sat on the floor of the café for a few minutes, bodies slumped at the tables as the reconstruction team tried to figure out how best to put the place back together.

When I stood up I felt a stabbing pain in my left calf. A large shard of glass was sticking out of it. I ignored it, keeping my weight on the other leg as I limped out.

Linus sat on the far side of the intersection, past the remains of the newsstand, facing the back of the rotunda. I sat beside him. After a few minutes of silence Linus, who hadn't smoked in ten years, asked me for a cigarette.

"I quit."

He nodded. "I suppose that's good. Hell of a time to do it, though. You know you should get that leg looked at."

"Yeah, I can't pull the glass out until I get to the clinic or else it'll just bleed worse. I know a good place that'll take care of it."

Linus reached for a pack of cigarettes that lay in the debris of the shattered newsstand. He put one in his mouth and lit it. "Don't mess with some third-rate bull," he puffed. "You can write it off if you let Recon do it. They'll want to control the perception, so you should get a good deal."

"I'll be fine."

"Suit yourself."

I could smell the tobacco through the burnt gunpowder and detonite, and I suddenly needed a smoke too.

"Kabul?" I asked.

"Yep."

It wasn't right. It wasn't wrong. Kabul hadn't committed a crime or done anything immoral. It was simply a part of the negotiation, placing their thumb on the scale—forcing Ackerman to pay so much to drive Kabul out that it might just be easier to let them compete. A suicide bomber just cost less than doing nothing.

"How'd they get him?"

"Snipers," said Linus. "There's at least a dozen snipers covering the square around the clock. With so many HighCon assets here, it's a tempting target... Our boys did their jobs, we're all good."

In the background I could hear the perception team. Corbett had already arrived, and was haggling over how to best shape the incident and who should get credit for what. Already they had come down to two intriguing but mutually exclusive possibilities—they could laud Ackerman security forces for stopping the bomber before he reached his target, or argue that he could've been stopped sooner if MidCons stopped bellyaching about unfair security tariffs.

"Maybe," said Collin's young voice, "we should have the reconstruction team rebuild the café exactly as it was, pretend like none of this happened."

"What? And ignore this opportunity! That's criminal!" shouted Corbett, pulling out his ledger and writing up an impromptu report.

I closed my eyes. Corbett was right, he'd own this noob before the year was out—if the kid didn't end up in prison first.

Linus was still smoking, but nobody dared hassle him about it. And despite the horror, I saw a ray of hope, from someone I had not expected.

"You saved a lot of lives today," I said.

Linus shook his head. "No, Charles, I protected our assets. It's the mitigation clause in every Ackerman contract. I had to."

"No, that wasn't mitigation. You took charge, you led us. You saved lives. The world is a better place because of what you did."

Linus sighed and took another drag. He was exhausted, and resented having to spend the energy to try one last time to explain.

"I don't see how you can miss this, Charles. You don't get it, even now. It's my job to know first aid, to help assets in trouble, to protect Ackerman and mitigate damage to it whenever I can. I did my job, I did it well, and I expect to be paid commensurate with the quality of my work. And I will be.

"We're assets, you and I. But you have this sentimentality; you seem to think that life should offer more. Well, I don't know about what should be. I just know that this is the way it is. We got caught in the crossfire of a rather tough negotiation today. That's all. Don't look for any more meaning than that. All that awaits idealists who can't stomach a harsh reality is disappointment, misery, and death. You should want more than that for yourself.

"I'm happy with the way things turned out. I'm happy because I believe in Nash. I will never get those responsible for this, I'll never meet them. But my colleagues will, rest assured. This will cost Kabul everything. I trust my colleagues. I did my job today, and tomorrow an Ackerman sniper will do his. If we all keep doing our jobs, Kabul will be gone, it's that simple."

He stood up, took a final deep draw and then tossed the cigarette aside. "This should clue you into the real world, Charles. This is what happens if you let your guard down, even for a second. Everyone, the entire world, is either with us or against us. They want to divide us, like the two prisoners. That is Nash.

"You did well today. You took direction in less than ideal circumstances. I'm proud of you, and you should be proud of yourself. You honestly could make Gamma. It's a shame you don't really try. In any case, you saved her life—I think. And you'll be paid well for it, I'll see to that."

It was with that that Linus, torn clothes and covered in blood, walked away. I looked up into the sky, one of the few clear blue skies I had seen all year. War had come to Ackerman.

14

Kate tended my wounds as I sat in a chair in the middle of her living room.

"Seems like I'm always cleaning you up."

I nodded, though I wasn't really listening.

"You okay?" she asked.

"I just can't believe Linus. The people he saved, they meant nothing to him. They were just assets."

"He's lean, sculpted by years of corporate work. He doesn't have emotions anymore. No fear, no sadness. He doesn't hesitate, he doesn't regret his decisions, he just acts. That's why he loves poker so much, why he's so good at it."

"I hate poker."

"Of course you do, you hate lying. You wear your heart on your sleeve. Poker is all about deception. People think 'cuz there's dice, it's random. But it's not. The odds are always the same. And everyone knows that you bet high on a good hand, and low on a bad one, so everyone tries to deceive you by doing the opposite. But we all know that everybody knows, and so on. So in the end it's the best liar who wins, the person who can most convince you of the weakness of his roll."

"He said that Nash supports corporations…"

"That's what all corporate agents say," she laughed. "He wasn't against them, but he said that, for the best success, trust had to be balanced equally with competition. Do you trust *any* of your colleagues?"

The stitches on my calf were neat, the bandages tight. Out in the wilds of LowCon were no hospitals to speak of, and experience was the best first aid. They had their own education.

"I've had enough. I can't go back. I'm done, Katherine. I can't work for Ackerman anymore."

"I know, hon. I know it's hard. Just keep working there a little longer."

"Longer? What on earth do I need to go back there for? My life is a joke, it's fake, and it doesn't mean anything! I'm never going back."

"I know, I know. But they own your futures. They'll come after you."

"Let them. They'll never find me here. If I cash everything out, move out here, I can drop my ledger into a river and…."

"Charlie, you can't," she cried.

"Oh, no. I didn't mean… I didn't mean to presume I was going to come *here*. I can get my own place."

"It's fine if you move in here with me. That's not what I meant. You can't quit Ackerman. Not yet."

"But you can show me. I can steal water, grow food, you can teach me to survive."

"You just can't," she pleaded. "You have to keep working."

"What are you talking about?"

She clasped her hand over her mouth. Her eyes were wide and she began to cry.

"I can't tell you," she said.

The woman who had never been frightened by anything looked at me as if I were already dead, as though my death was a certainty no one could avoid.

"What have you done?" I said.

"It's not me, Charlie."

"Your friends. Oh my god, are they going to turn me in? I should have…."

"No, it's not them, Charlie, please!"

"Why can't I leave Ackerman?"

She still refused to answer.

"I have to leave. It doesn't matter where I go, but I can't stay there. You have to understand that."

She shook her head. "It's over, Charlie."

"What? You're leaving me because I'm going to quit work?"

"No. Ackerman is over. They're through. Everybody is. Corporations, the world, it's coming to an end. It's going to crash. It's all over."

I laughed.

She had gotten me worked up over nothing. We had spent so much time in her world that I sometimes forgot how little she knew about mine.

"There are crashes all the time," I said, reassuringly. "It's a part of business."

She fell to the couch and held her head in her hands.

"No, you don't understand. Everything, the entire system. Every corporation, every colleague—everything is going to go bankrupt."

"Not everything. Ackerman certainly won't," I chuckled. "They're too big; they're insulated from problems like that. It's called diversification. You may know governments, but I know corporations, and I hate to tell you, but nothing is ever going to end Ackerman."

She choked and shook her head. She couldn't look me in the eye.

"They're the cause of the problem. And it's not *going* to happen. It's already happened. Ackerman is dead, they just don't know it yet."

"Whoa, I was there this morning. They're fine. I don't know what you think you know, or what someone told you...."

"Nobody told me anything."

"I'm telling you, it's not possible."

"I'm sure that's what governments thought—'It's a crash, like any other.' But crashes get worse each time. The people willing to risk or sacrifice the most will probably win, and so the line of acceptable behavior moves closer and closer to mutually assured destruction. Everyone keeps wagering more and more until everything is leveraged, and then the system dies."

"What are you talking about?"

She breathed deeply and began. "Ten years ago we had a really cold year, and ice began encroaching into habitable land. Land prices shot up."

"Yeah, but it was an off year. The next year was warmer and the ice receded."

"Yes, but land prices never came back down. That initial increase sparked massive speculation on the market. So many people were buying land that they artificially inflated the price, fueling more speculation. I mean, land is real, right? Not like paper money. So they thought it was a sure thing. Land prices got so high that everybody wanted in on the boom, making the boom even larger. The reality of how much land was actually available didn't make a difference. People wanted it because everybody else wanted it.

"Ackerman saw a huge opportunity there. They got in early, and they got in big. They figured out that if they put everything they had into land—that simply by investing in land—they could cause the price to go up even more. It was like printing money. Buying more land made the land they had more valuable.

Page 148

"But that only works if the prices keep going up, so they had to keep putting more money in it. They started selling the futures of the land they were buying to buy even more. They were taking out loans against property they didn't even own yet."

"Who on earth would lend them the money to do that?"

"They're Ackerman! Who in their right mind thinks Ackerman can't pay back a debt? It's the largest corp in human history. And when other people saw them doing this, they said, 'Hey, no corp would be that stupid, they must know something we don't!' and they all jumped on the bandwagon. The price of land went up four hundred percent in three years."

"I remember this—the bubble burst after that. This all happened years ago," I said. "If Ackerman had actually done all of that, they'd have gone bankrupt."

"They did."

I waited, but she didn't say anything else.

"What do you mean, they did?"

"Ackerman went bankrupt about five years ago."

"Kate, I work there every day. I'm telling you, they're financially sound. Christ, Ackerman has the most solid financial foundation of any corporation in history."

"That's Perception Management talking. Takashi knew that if people learned how bad Ackerman had been hit, they'd make all their margin calls and Ackerman would be wiped out. So he hid the debt, and just started kicking the can down the road."

"You can't hide debt like that!"

"Sure you can. Just keep moving it around."

"Look, we may have lost some money in real estate, but we're a brokerage firm, and we're making record profits in Arbitrage."

"That's where it's hidden," Kate said. "The entire debt is just washed out over the trading floor. Takashi ordered trade quotas raised by fifty percent and gave huge bonuses to anybody who doubled their previous earnings. Well, you can't get blood from a stone, so traders from Ackerman offices all over the world are simply trading to each other. Ten million rolls of toilet paper in Guam are sold to Ackerman offices in Paris, then to New Washington, and then back to Guam. They get traded three times in one day and never leave the warehouse, and all of those sales count as revenue coming in. And the traders are all getting record commissions on these phantom trades."

"But there would be no real money coming in," I said. "Somebody would have noticed that."

"Nobody noticed when they were doing the same thing with land. Money is coming in; it's just coming from future trades nobody's yet made. On paper, every phantom trade looks as though it brings in money. But in reality it costs the corporation money in commissions and services. Since they didn't have the money for a real trade in the first place, they can't pay for the phantom one, so every five phantom trades executed this month requires another eight next month to pay for. The trading floor doesn't even do real trades anymore; they don't have the time for it. They're the hardest working division in Ackerman and their only job is to hide debt, to try to purchase fewer losses this month than they did last."

I couldn't even feel the gash in my leg or the cuts on my face. Her revelation was stronger than any painkiller. I fell back into my chair.

"At this point they're just in a state of denial. They can't fathom a world without Ackerman. They really believe something will come to save them if they can hold off the grim reaper just a little bit longer. They can't believe that, collectively, they'd do something that stupid, so they must not have. They figure that someone has a way out of all this, that some colleague out there has a plan to rescue them. So they keep gaming the system, get as much money before the problem is fixed. Hey, they're making so much on commissions that it can't possibly be wrong, right?"

"So Ackerman is going to fail?"

"Yep."

As the reality set in, my fear melted, and I felt an overwhelming sense of joy. Everyone thinks themselves above petty revenge, but there was justice in this. All those people, everyone at Ackerman who thought themselves masters of the universe, who bought and sold lives for pennies on the dollar, they were all about to be taught one hell of a lesson.

"Why are you smiling?"

"Don't you see? We're going to be free! Ackerman can't come after us if they're bankrupt! This is all the more reason to leave, get out while the getting's good! This is wonderful!"

"Oh my god, Charlie, I don't think you understand what I'm saying."

"I understand perfectly! Ackerman can't hurt us. This is great!"

"No. The problem started in land. More than eighty percent of all corporations at the time had something invested in real-estate, and probably a third of those were hit hard enough by the correction to go bankrupt. Less than five percent of them actually failed. So what the hell happened to the debt?"

"Well I don't know. But the corporations survived, so it must have gone somewhere."

"Well, that's what you said about Ackerman. Every one of those corporations say that they made all their money back. But if Ackerman—one of the most powerful corporations in the world—couldn't squeeze a dime out of the market to save themselves, what makes you think any of the other corporations could?"

I had lived through two bombings, the death of my father, and the untold suffering I watched in the executions every month. None of it prepared me for how empty I felt at that moment.

"Everybody's doing it?" I asked.

"About a third of our Karitzu at least. It's harder to tell for some of the others, especially those based in Europa. They're running schemes like this everywhere; it was the only way for them to compete, to survive—at least for another day."

"You're telling me a third of these corporations are going to fail?"

"No. I'm telling you that they already have. These corps exist only on paper; they don't even own their own colleagues anymore. They just don't know it yet."

I had to think like Linus. He would be able to understand the enormity of it. It's always been theoretically possible for man to destroy himself. We always think it won't happen on our watch, that it will be some other generation that destroys the world. That, in the end, is what makes us blind to the possibility, which is the very thing that makes it possible.

But capitalism is a game of brinksmanship, survival by being willing to risk just slightly more than your competitor is. Of course the world would come to this, with both sides driving themselves (and everybody else) off a cliff. Was there any other way?

All that really surprised me was that it hadn't ever crossed my mind until then.

So what would be the next logical step? What would Linus say would come next?

There would be a tipping point, a point at which the phantom trades could no longer be kept secret. Massive layoffs would follow within days; corporations would fail overnight. Within a week we could see a third of all corps—at least in the Americas, and possibly across the world—collapse. And this would not be any third, but the largest third—those that had leveraged the most. Even to an Epsilon the ramifications were clear—you'd see half of the remaining corporations wiped out completely, corporations that had done nothing wrong, that had not shared in the risk, would be sharing in the consequences.

"The PulpMill Paper Company," she said, "has never invested in anything other than exactly what they need to run their business. Everything they do is above board. But sixty percent of their business comes directly from Ackerman, and the rest of it from within the Karitzu. When Ackerman fails, PulpMill will go under, too. The cost of paper will soar. Any corporation with narrow margins—which is just about all of them—won't be able to buy any. So they'll go under. In a two-week period more than half the jobs on two continents are going to vanish. The price of everything will skyrocket. Everyone will pull their money from the system—a run on every bank in the world, simultaneously. Credit will freeze up; corporations won't be able to make their payrolls. Even if they could, caps would become worthless, and food and water will be the only thing of value—but there won't even be close to enough of that to go around."

"What do you mean?"

"The Al-Arabina Karitzu controls over eighty percent of the world's oil. They're heavily invested in Ackerman. If Arabina fails, the flow of oil and gasoline stops completely. How are you going to supply food to a city without trucks? We can't get water without pumps, which need oil. Without coal there's no electricity. And even if you had trucks, who's going to pay the truck drivers? And with what?"

"There must... if this is really happening, there must be a way to stop it."

She nodded. "I understand how you feel. I've known this for a while, so sometimes I forget what it's like to hear it for the first time.

"You know, light travels so fast that we think it's instantaneous. But it's not. It has an actual speed. Over long distances, you can measure it. The light from the sun takes eight minutes to get here. What we see in the sky isn't the sun as it is, but as it was eight minutes ago. If it exploded, or just vanished, we'd still see it. Nobody would know, because we don't have a measuring device faster than the speed of light. We wouldn't know for eight minutes.

"You and I, the whole world, we're living now in those eight minutes. Ackerman, your colleagues, corps, the world as a whole—are all dead, they just don't see it yet. We are waiting on the day before the dinosaurs went extinct. We know for certain that it'll happen, but there's nothing we can possibly do about it. The age of corporations is over, my love."

15

Kate pulled a small tea infuser out of the cupboard. She crushed up some leaves, put them into it, and dropped it into a clay mug. Then she put a dollop of condensed milk into the tea.

It was a precious commodity, the milk. But I had lost my appetite.

"Is this what they would call a war?" I asked.

"War is the inevitable conclusion of capitalism. We've been at war for centuries. This is the end of war.

"Corporations are run by people, nothing more or less. They're not monsters, not superhuman intellects, just people who are, for the most part, reasonably as clever as one another. Some corporations will fail and others succeed. But everyone thinks that they deserve to win. So when they think they're going to lose, they feel justified in moving the line of acceptable behavior further down the field. They resort to more and more desperate actions to survive. Those desperate actions become the norm, and the next corporation has to take even more drastic measures just to compete."

"But that's so selfish."

"That's capitalism. Survival of the fittest. A good capitalist will tell you that in general people are ethical and would never take advantage of the system. That's what the Communists thought, too. Zino hated this kind of behavior. She assumed most people would never do it. She said that if your actions were honest, all you needed was the rational perception of others. But that's not true. They need to be honest, too. Sure, on paper competition is survival of the fittest; the smartest and most efficient corporation wins. But really the winner is the one who can *appear* to be the best while actually investing the least in customers or other expenses, the one who can betray the most people with the fewest knowing about it—the one who can best ignore human conscience without getting caught. Given unrestricted power, the corporation will feel entitled, even obligated, to leverage it. Unrestricted competition is a policy of scorched earth, period.

"The same was true for governments, too. Power was supposed to be shared."

My hand was trembling as I brought the tea to my lips. "We have to warn people."

"How? Most people in the corporation don't even know a crash is coming. They won't until it's too late. Those who do are already making preparations to run, and the last thing they want to do is tell anyone else. You talk, and Ackerman will arrest you. Perception Management will call it a scare tactic to make money by forcing a run on banks or selling short, and everyone—even Perception itself—will believe it."

"Kate, do you know how many people are going to die?"

"Most. It'll be mass famine."

"This can't be true, it just can't be."

"I wish it weren't. As much as I hate Ackerman, nobody deserves this. But this is why I hate them, because this is what they bring us. The victors of competition haven't ever shared their profits, but they're happy to share their losses."

"I'm saying it can't. You must be wrong."

Kate shook her head. "I wish we were. We're not."

Now that I had come most to respect life, I was going to witness the loss of it on an unparalleled scale.

But wait. She told me. Why would she tell me if nothing can be done? She wants me to stay at Ackerman. That could only matter if....

"You built one!" I cried. "An actual republic! You really are a citizen. You saw this coming years ago, and you've been preparing. That's what the secret meetings have been about, that's what you've been hiding from me."

A look of joy bloomed—as if a terrible burden was lifted. She could never tell me, never violate that oath. But now that I knew....

"I wanted to tell you so much. It's never been so hard to keep a secret. But so much is at stake, and there are a lot of us. The only thing that can get us killed is if they find out before we're ready. If they do, they'll take the bunker."

"Bunker?"

She turned to me. "Yeah, an old bunker under one of the old apartment buildings up at Glendale. We found it by accident; it's not on any map, and there's no reference to it in the Galt or any of the ruins. It's from the last, great republic. It was designed for a nuclear war—it's huge. We've been stocking it for years—food, water; we have solar generators, hydroponics, waste reclamation and management. We can live down there for decades."

"We? How many people?"

"About a thousand. It's a vault. Once the doors are sealed, not even Ackerman could get inside—if they were still around."

I loved Kate; nothing was more important to me than she was. But I was overwhelmed with fear. The pain from my panic attacks, which I hadn't felt since I met her, came flooding back. I was a man on a sinking ship who's been told only one lifeboat is left.

"If... if somebody wanted to get in, how would he do it?"

"We all have tickets—every family."

"But you don't have family."

"They gave me two tickets, one for me and one for someone else."

My throat thickened again, and I couldn't breathe. "Who are you taking?" I croaked.

She gave a playful little laugh and rubbed her foot against my side. "You really don't know?"

"Well, we haven't been together that long. You have a lot of friends—"

"Of course I'm taking you, Charlie. Don't be silly."

I grabbed her by the waist and began spinning her through the air. She giggled and laughed. I wanted to ask her thousands of questions. But between the blast at the café, learning that the world was coming to an end, and this refuge of salvation, I was exhausted.

That night we lay in bed, but I couldn't sleep, overcome with torrents of emotion: crushed at the thought of so much suffering, guilty that part of me thought that they deserved it, elated that I might survive, and unworthy of the honor. I was even a little angry with Kate; she'd passed on a horrible burden, and a terrible risk. The lives of the other thousand citizens, the fate of the Republic, were not worth risking over a colleague like me.

"Jazelle agreed to let me in?" I joked.

"She did," chuckled Kate, "but I don't think she likes you. She thinks you could be Retention. After the crash, it won't much matter."

I could have been Retention. Jazelle had a point. And anyway, if I had learned about the Republic, Ackerman could too. Heck, every colleague is Retention, by definition.

Corporatism breeds paranoia.

I tried to quiet my mind.

I would never tell, of course. Ackerman could torture me until the end of time (or at least until the crash) and I would never tell.

But I was also racked with guilt over even having gotten the information out of her. How much she must have sacrificed with her citizen friends by falling in love with a colleague. I mourned the loss of the world, the walking dead who knew nothing about their future. But as Kate said, we had to focus on what we could control, not what we couldn't. We would live, and that was something.

Maybe we all have a little colleague in each of us.

"It'll be so wonderful to live in a republic, free of all corruption."

Kate laughed. "Oh, my darling, I wish that were true. Republics had corruption, too, people trying to grab money and power. They don't incentivize corruption as such, but people will try to game any system. The difference is that in a republic, power is distributed more evenly. The system isn't one dollar one vote, but one man, one vote. The rich will be more powerful than the poor, they always are, and maybe it's supposed to be that way. But the fate of each is tied more proportionately to the other, and that helps keep the peace.

"But the only real check against corruption is vigilance. The lack of it lead to the death of republics: success bred complacency and arrogance, just like today. They thought that the system was enough to protect them, that they didn't need to be involved. The point of a republic was to elect people to run government for you so you could live your life. But citizens just let go of the rope. Nobody voted, nobody got educated on the complexities of the governing. And the corporations moved in and spent massive amounts of money on perception, promoting the people that they wanted into office, and convincing the public that the rich should get richer, so that they could employ the poor and drive the economy. They convinced people that capitalism—this god of nature—would do the oversight for them, that the free hand of the market would keep them safe. But it wasn't true, and on that front, the corporatists and I agree—life is work."

"I can't believe I never have to go back to Ackerman."

"Oh Charlie, oh no. You have to go back."

"What?"

"Don't you see? If you don't, they'll come looking for you."

"I, but—"

"Charlie, this is not negotiable. I wasn't even supposed to tell you—not for a few weeks, but since you said you were going to quit working, I had to. Your coming here every night is bad enough, but as long as they think you're going to pay them back, they don't care. If you stop going in to work, they'll come here, and in force. They'll arrest people, bring them in, start asking questions."

"I'm sorry, Kate. How can I go back? I am not a colleague anymore. I can't live that life."

Her eyes were sad. "I understand. But you have to anyway. You said that you wanted a way to redeem yourself—for Sarah."

I knew what was coming.

"You have no idea," she said, "no idea how hard I've worked to convince them to let you keep coming here. I've been cut out of nearly all of the decisions—they won't talk to me or come here to meet with me. And that's okay, but I can't give you any more."

"This is cruel."

"I know," she said. "Let's go back together. I'll live at your place. But you can't stop going to work or meeting with Linus. If you've been looking for a way to prove yourself, this is it. You have to go back."

She would go back with me, too. I knew that. That arrangement would help. But she was the only beautiful thing in my life.

I would go back to Ackerman. I would do carry the burden for Sarah Aisling. I had asked for the chance to be like her, to take risks like her, to stand up for what I believed. But I had wanted to do so on my terms. Would that life were like that, challenging us in the time and place of our choosing. No, I had to go back to Ackerman, precisely because it was the last thing I wanted to do.

"How long until the crash?" I asked.

"There's no way to know. As it gets closer we've gotten better at pinning it down. Our best guess is it's about four to eight weeks away. But a single bad market fluctuation could catalyze an entire catastrophe overnight."

I shifted uncomfortably.

"We'll know a day or two before it gets bad. That's why I've been having you stay here at night. At the first sign of serious trouble in the market, you should come straight here. We go to the bunker together. Once they seal it up, Ackerman will never hurt us again."

I had survived two bombings already, and now I saw myself getting entombed in the center of Capital City while the economy itself detonated.

She put both hands on my face and looked me in the eyes. "If you don't get out of the city, I will go in," she said. "I will find you. Do you understand me? I will not leave you out here alone."

"No," I said. "You'd never find me, and I don't want you to miss the vault. Whatever happens, I'll be okay if I know you're safe."

"I'm not going into the vault without you."

"No, Kate. It's a deal-breaker. I won't go back unless you promise me that you won't come after for me."

"Once they close those doors, they're not opening for decades. Promise me you won't miss it."

"I won't."

16

I sat at my desk, massaging my right leg. It ached, and I could tell even before I checked the weather futures that we were in for a storm. There was a hurricane coming, and everybody was hustling to finish as much work as they could before hunkering down for the night. It was hard to fake interest in a single storm, no matter how big it was. Bernard, Corbett, Leoben, all my colleagues were huffing around, trying to negotiate supplies to last a couple of days in case the power went out. In a couple of months they'd all be corpses. They'd have no food, no water, and no electricity. The building would be a mausoleum.

I logged into my terminal. I found an escrow credit of 13,861.44 caps, for emergency mitigation services rendered at the café. I also found a press release, which read that a Kabul suicide bomber attacked Atlas Square, but was shot and killed before he could reach his target. A preliminary investigation showed that spies inside Ackerman had helped him infiltrate the square undetected. Already the CEO was preparing proposals to ferret these traitors out, and was personally going to oversee a new economic offensive against Kabul Coffee.

I still hadn't received my commission from my Aisling report.

I had only managed a few reports by lunch. I had always said that nothing was worse than administrative paperwork. But paperwork under the futility of an impending Armageddon, that would crush the spirit of even the stoutest of actuaries.

"The storm won't be that bad," scoffed Corbett. "These people. You need battery backups, backup routers, generators. They call themselves professionals? The whole city could go dark, and I'd still be working. Nobody here is dedicated, not one iota."

Bernard hastily ripped open a bag of candies and sent them flying all over the room. With a grunt he fell to his hands and knees and began picking them up, popping the occasional one into his mouth when he thought nobody was looking.

"Bernard, that's disgusting!" Corbett said. He turned to me. "I saw you at the café yesterday. Didn't want to trouble you. You had one hell of an afternoon. How did you like our crafting of the incident? I hope it meets with your approval."

I nodded.

"Oh, they're going to add a two and a half percent levy to cover the war," groaned Bernard. "How will I ever cope with it? I've barely got enough to live on as it is."

"Cope?" Corbett said. "You should be counting your blessings, you ungrateful pig! Not many CEOs could wage an effective war at two and-a-half percent. Christ, Bernard, Charles was nearly killed. These Kabul people are maniacs. All this over coffee? Obviously they can't handle legitimate competition. We need to kill them all, every one. Hell, we should have done this last month! How do we expect to stay competitive if we let some piss-ant company like Kabul walk all over us?"

"Oh, there are plenty of ways to get 'em without having to charge *me* a security fee," grumbled Bernard "I don't go to places like Atlas Square precisely for this reason. Let the HighCons deal with HighSec, if they're stupid enough to all gather in one spot!"

"They have a right to have a place of their own, where they can engage in civil discourse and debate. What are you, a communist? Your lack of sympathy for your own colleagues is disgusting!" Corbett exclaimed.

"Takashi could have done better," Bernard said.

"What?" stammered Corbett.

"I mean… well, you know what I mean. If I were advising Takashi, I'd have told him to just let Kabul in. We have got bigger fish to fry."

"You're a coward, Bernard!"

"That's it. You called me a pig and I let it go because you're a colleague, but no more. I'm going to sue you for slander!"

I returned to my cubicle. I found a memo reminding me that colleagues who left their windows open during the storm would suffer stiff fines, and that any equipment damaged as a result of a lightning strike would be the sole responsibility of the owner. As I tossed it into the trash, Corbett snuck in behind me.

"Charles, old boy, I have something for you. I was going to give it to you yesterday, but…."

"Not now."

"Twenty caps. You can make a mint on this. Come on, you know I'm good."

I shook my head.

"Okay, ten caps, but I won't go that low next time."

I took the offer.

"Leoben is retiring. He's gone."

I could make a few caps off that, for sure. Leoben was a department head. A day or two before retirement, managers would always fire their staff and auction off the most valuable equipment, boost short-term profits, goose the stock before they sold their options. I thanked him, but if Corbett knew, so did everyone else—it would be too late to get in on it. Besides, what would be the point?

It had only been five hours and already I couldn't bear it. I couldn't endure another week, let alone a month or two.

Maybe there are signs. If I can predict more accurately, figure out exactly when this is going to happen....

I worked inside the firm, with far more access to information than Kate and her colleagues. I was sure I'd be able to get better insight on when the collapse would hit.

The futures market, I figured that was the way to tell. They placed completely unregulated bets on the future value of commodities. The only people who made any money were the ones who researched like crazy, cheated better than the next guy, or had insider information.

I browsed Ackerman's stock and futures prices. They were all within the norms, no hint of the coming crash. Some wackos were making outrageous bets on Ackerman suddenly collapsing or rising meteorically, but people did that every day. I checked to see if Linus' name showed up on any bets anywhere—if anyone would know where Ackerman was headed, he would. Nothing.

When the crash hit, it was going to be fast.

I was sick of not being able to see clearly and turned on the master cubicle light. I refocused my efforts, checking the futures of oil, water, air, even of CEO Takahiro Takashi himself. I found nothing unusual.

"What the hell are you doing?" cried Bernard, bursting into the cubicle. "You're wasting light!"

"I've paid for it."

"It looks bad!"

"Fine, if it really means that much to you, my wallet is on the desk, take a twenty."

His eyes lit up. He looked around suspiciously before snatching a twenty.

I was getting nowhere. By the time the crash was big enough to be reflected in futures, it would be too late. The answer was the phantom trades. That would be the flashpoint where the crash would hit first.

"Is... is that trading stats?" he asked me.

"Yeah."

"What are you doing?"

"Trading."

"On the Ackerman floor? Oh my god," he laughed. "What do you know about Arbitrage? You're going to get killed. I swear, I'm going to short your futures. I'll make a killing! You'll owe Ackerman for the rest of your life."

He walked out laughing. My futures—in all the excitement I had fallen out of the habit of checking them.

When I did I nearly fell out of my chair. Once worth more than forty caps apiece, they were down to little more than two cents.

Ackerman knew.

If they were just upset that I had been visiting LowSec, I'd expect a loss of about five or ten caps. But the whole Arbitrage division—Christ, maybe even all of Ackerman— had decided that I was a bad bet. It was impossible to know how much they knew about Kate, or our Republic. But the consensus on the trading floor was that I had no future.

Retention was probably already surveilling me. They wouldn't let my stock fall to nothing without finding some way of getting their money back. But now that I had checked, I knew, and whatever value I had to them was over.

They'd be coming.

If they arrested me, I was dead—if not on the gallows, then starving in jail after the crash.

I swept my keyboard and terminal completely off my desk and jumped up on top of it. I could see over the partitions to the elevators. The doors were opening, and several men wearing the fine suits reserved for Retention agents walked onto the floor. They spotted me, and I ducked back down.

I would have to get out of Capital City. My only immediate advantage was that the maze of seventh floor cubicles was almost organic. Divisions and partitions were constantly merging and splitting. Years of dodging Bernard in that labyrinth had taught me every recess, every nook.

I grabbed my ledger and burst out of my cubicle. The nearest fire exit was around the corner and down the hall. I caught a colleague as he was coming from his office, knocking him back through a partition, tossing papers everywhere. In the chaos I grabbed another partition and brought it down into the hallway.

I reached the exit and waved my ledger over the terminal.

"Charles Thatcher," chimed a gentle computer voice. "Please remain where you are. Authorities will be with you shortly."

Already my ledger had been disconnected. I wouldn't be able to open doors, make electronic business transactions, or even get past the most elementary security.

I saw a mail clerk. I ran towards him, and, sprinting over his cart, slipped my ledger into one of the side pockets.

I turned into another cubicle, and crashed through another partition. It fell in a heap with two more, and I clambered through them and down the aisle. This mess would slow Retention down, but nothing would stop them.

I reached the snack room, where I found a number of colleagues. Bernard was up to his elbows in freshly purchased chocolate bars.

"Charles? What do *you* want?" he said, spewing wafer crusts from his mouth.

I grabbed his tie and pulled him into a punch. I hit his face—once, twice, then a third time. He squealed and fell back, blood pouring everywhere.

"You stole my twenty, you fat bastard!" I cried, reaching into his suit. I pulled out his wallet and took all the cash in it, but as I did I also snuck his ledger, and quickly slid it into my own pocket. I tossed the wallet onto him.

"I catch you near my things again, and you're dead!" I shouted, giving him a kick before running out. With any luck, the brutality of my attack would keep him from noticing his ledger was missing.

As I made my way toward the elevators, a commotion broke out ahead of me. I ducked into a tiny corner—an awkward space made from the juxtaposition of two cubicles that weren't quite lined up, like a hole in the universe. I heard the pounding of feet, and watched as two agents ran past me towards the break room.

I dashed to the elevator. Waving Bernard's ledger over the terminal, the doors opened, and I clambered inside. I jabbed the lobby button again and again, suffering agonizing moments waiting for the doors to close. They did, and I began the slow ride down all seven flights.

It was stupid to take the elevator—at any moment security could lock it off. But the stairs were located on the other side of the building; I'd never have made it. At last the doors opened at the lobby. I hurried past the guard at Simon's old desk and ran out into the courtyard.

The sulfur was already strong in the air, and the wind was picking up. I jogged to the main thoroughfare, where I was able to flag down a cab.

I piled in. Bernard's face flashed on the driver's terminal, but he didn't bother to look at it.

"Where to?"

"The Galt."

The cab pulled away and merged into the traffic. With any luck they'd be following the mail cart for a little while.

I had a few moments to myself, and that's when I noticed the pain in my chest. I clutched it, and once again reached for my pills, which I had long thrown out.

I'm not dying. It's in your mind, push it out.

I repeated it over and over. Every panic attack feels as if it's the last one, as if this time it's a real heart attack. I could see the sky, the open air, but somehow felt like I was back at Allenhurst. I wondered if I was still there, under the weight of the building. Maybe I had never gotten out, the years since just the hallucinations of a dying man.

Am I alive?

I took deep breaths. The running was over, and I'd be safe once I snuck into the Galt, at least for a little while.

I certainly didn't want to go there—a public place. My first instinct was to head straight to Kate's. If anybody could hide me, she could.

But I had no idea what Ackerman knew.

I had been acting suspiciously for some time, giving Corbett, Bernard, and even Linus reasons to report me.

If they knew about Kate, they might be waiting there for me. If not, I could lead them there. Hopefully they were headed to LowSec in force, trying to get there before I warned her. With some luck, they would draw enough attention that Kate and her friends could all escape to the vault, where nobody would see or hear from them for half a century.

And that was the rosiest end I could imagine.

Retention could have paid Bernard to drop a fake report in my lap, on the off chance they might make some cash, especially if they were already wary of me. But it could have been far simpler than that. Maybe they'd disseminated hundreds of fake Aisling reports across the territory, and then set up a rental office to see who stops by.

The plot seemed too intricate, too complicated. No doubt that's what Evans thought.

I arrived at the Galt. I figured Bernard could pay for expedited service, and I passed through security almost immediately.

I sat at a computer terminal and began looking up my futures. If they had been going down steadily over the last week or so, I might have a reason to hope. But if they fell immediately after meeting Kate, my fate was pretty much sealed. I got into the Ackerman database just fine, but all of my records had been restricted, and Bernard's ledger didn't have nearly enough credit to get around it.

I leaned back in my chair. If they hadn't figured out by now that I had his ledger, they would soon.

Then I remembered the phantom trades.

If everything had been a setup from the very beginning, I could live with that. I'd be reclamated for sure, but that would be fine. It was the not knowing that was tearing me up. I could live with the lie. I couldn't live with the doubt.

If I could find the phantom trades, then the world was coming to an end, but Kate had been real, and she might have escaped. If they weren't real, then there was no collapse, no Republic, no citizens—just the diabolically brilliant minds of Ackerman Retention, a species of man that could both love their corporation while at the same time lambast the absurdity and hypocrisy of it all.

I began poring over Ackerman's trading records, but I couldn't make heads or tails of it. It was encrypted in the language of arbitrage, a cipher I couldn't read. I began printing as many of the records as I could. I needed a professional trader.

I was packing up the printouts when two security guards approached me. I gritted my teeth. I couldn't see any weapons on them, but they'd be armed. There was no running for it; security could lock the entire building down in a second.

"Mr. Thatcher?"

I didn't say anything.

"Mr. Thatcher, the Director of Community Relations would like to speak with you."

17

I stood in a tall, octagonal chamber. Thirty-foot-high cherry wood bookcases with wrought iron railings lined the walls. Ornate red and gold drapes hung from the ceiling and over the windows. In the center of the room at cherry desk, sat a kindly looking man wearing reading glasses. He looked up from his report and smiled courteously.

"Mr. Thatcher, good afternoon," he said, standing to shake my hand. "It's a pleasure to meet you."

I didn't reply.

"I'm sorry to inconvenience you," he continued, "but I'm afraid we have a bit of a problem. We've been contacted by the Ackerman Brothers Securities and Investments firm. It appears that they want you on suspicion of several crimes committed against them."

I looked down at the floor. He had nice shoes.

"They believe you are in the building, and requested that we hand you over to them."

"I see."

"Indeed. Now, I'm sure that this is all a misunderstanding between you and the firm, and that you're as eager as anyone to see it all cleared up. But it's our policy never to hand clients over to anyone."

I looked up at him.

"Now, they charge that you have taken the ledger of a colleague, a Mr. Bernard Milton. Indeed, that is the ledger you used to get into the building. They have not deactivated it, presumably so they can track you."

"I see."

"Quite. Now by whatever circumstances you came into possession of that ledger, I'm sure that they were legitimate. Nevertheless, its funds are limited, and once you can no longer afford to stay in this building, we will have to ask you to leave."

Neither he nor the guards seemed hesitant, or in the slightest bit nervous, which troubled me.

"Okay."

"Very well. Now that we understand the situation, let me tell you what we can offer you. We have several secret escape routes for just such an occasion. They are terribly expensive, far more than you can afford at present."

"I would assume so."

"However, this ledger may have a significant line of credit. If so, you would be able to purchase the use of one of our tunnels, and we would guarantee you safe passage out of here."

I scoffed. He must have thought I was a noob.

"They'll know you let me escape."

"What they'll know and what they can prove to the Karitzu are two different things. We'll claim you used the funds to bide your time while you escaped with Waste Management."

"Why do you need me? Why not just take the money from the ledger yourself?"

"A forensic analysis of the ledger could lead them to the physical person who used it. If you're the person taking out the loan, then we are not a party to any crime."

I chuckled. They *did* know what they were doing.

"They'll never let you keep Bernard's money," I said.

"They have no choice. Karitzu regulations on this are clear. The theft is considered to be of the ledger and the funds, Mr. Thatcher, not of our services. We will tell them that we charged the ledger in good faith. Since Ackerman failed to disable the ledger, the liability is theirs."

I looked at both the guards for some form of guidance or signal, but they were motionless, like statues, leaving the director and me alone in the room.

"Why would you help me?"

"I'm not. This is merely a service we provide. If you can't obtain the loan, or if the funds are insufficient, you will obviously be unable to avail yourself of it."

"How can I trust you'll do what you say?"

"We're a reputable firm, Mr. Thatcher. The Karitzu might be filled with crime and corruption, and I've no doubt Ackerman is. But the Galt prides itself on honesty and dependability."

This from a man looking to rip off Ackerman for as much as a hundred thousand caps.

"We've never turned over a customer's records or violated a contract. This is my contract with you."

I'd have had a hard time knowing what to do even with time to decide. But every second we spoke, funds were draining from Bernard's ledger.

I pulled out the tablet and began racking up loans, liquidating everything I could. Then I handed the device to the director. He swiped his card and tapped out a charge.

He watched, indifferently, as the transaction processed. Finally it bleated.

"Very good, Mr. Thatcher. I have a hundred caps for you, cash. That should help. We'll be keeping the ledger for

Ackerman Brothers. My agent, Mr. Thompson, will take you to the tunnels. I wish you the best of luck. We appreciate your business."

Mr. Thompson came out and motioned down a circular metal staircase and into a small room with a large vault door. He entered a code at the control panel, and a red light began to spin and a siren wailed.

I watched as a long forked arm came out, traveled along the wall and locked onto a pinion. The locks disengaged, the door popped off its mount, and the arm began rolling back into the wall. Behind where the door had been was a dark cavern.

"Thank you again, Mr. Thatcher."

I stepped into the rocky tunnel. The alarm wailed again, and the door slowly locked back into place behind me.

It was slow going. I was blind, no source of light at all. I stumbled along, using the cave walls for support. Even a single trip could be disastrous, I could lose my sense of direction and find myself headed back where I came from.

After a while I noticed a slight upward slope. I came to a huge metal grate wall, a jagged hole in it as if it had been blasted out. A faint light emanated from a manhole cover in the ceiling just beyond it. I climbed through the wall and into an underground structure. It was monstrous, wide enough for two cars. I walked down it, finding a manhole every couple hundred yards.

I traveled that way for two miles until I hit a dead end. It was a wall, and while it was pitch black, I was pretty sure that the wall was solid.

I wondered if I had missed a turn somewhere, or if this escape route was a trap. Maybe I was one of dozens of people sent down there to die. But feeling along I found a hatch. I opened it to find a small, dimly lit chamber. I climbed through, and the hatch fell closed behind me, locking shut.

The chamber was just big enough to hold an iron ladder. I climbed up and through another hatch, finding myself in a brick room with landscaping implements and a door. I stepped out of a maintenance shed in the middle of Browning Park.

I half-expected lights and sirens as I exited the building, but it was quiet. I felt alone, free. I had no ledger, mine or anyone else's, and for the first time in my life, nobody knew where I was.

The weather was getting pretty wild by now. The park, littered with twigs and smaller branches, was empty.

I hailed a taxi, but only had enough cash to get about two-thirds of the way to Linus' house. I walked the rest of the way, clutching the papers to my chest against the wind and rain. Darkness had fallen by the time I arrived at Ackerman's wealthy Red Oaks district and found Linus' home.

The wind was howling through the trees and branches were falling everywhere. All of the homes had lowered steel shutters over the windows and were powered from buried power lines or by generators. Like my first trip to LowSec, I didn't see a soul. The place looked abandoned. At least I didn't see any sign of police either. But they'd come. When, of course, depended on the severity of the charges against me. It was a bad storm, and with any luck Ackerman had more urgent matters than staking out every possible place I could go.

I rang the bell. Linus opened the door with a look of shock on his face—something I had never seen before.

"Charles, my god! You're soaking wet! How long have you been out there?"

"I walked."

"From your office? You shouldn't be out in this weather. I'd have loaned you the money if you needed cab."

"No, no. Something came up."

"Well, come in, make yourself at home. Take off your coat, let it dry. The rack is over there. My god, why didn't you at least wear a hat?"

"It doesn't matter."

"There's a storm coming—it's quite big. This is just the beginning. We're going to see some significant damage; roofs torn off, power lines out, the works. You should have waited until tomorrow."

"I can pay you a thousand caps for an hour. I need you to review some documents."

"Now? You're joking? You really want to spend a grand?"

I handed him the records. He held them away from him in disgust.

"These are soaked, I can barely read them. Most of them are completely ruined."

"A few of the pages are legible. I need you to go over them."

"What am I looking for?"

"Anything out of the ordinary. Maybe... well, I don't..."

I stopped talking and began looking around the room.

"Oh," Linus said, picking his drink up off the table. "Don't worry, I acquired a privacy clause in my contract when I became a Gamma. Ackerman can't tap my home without a warrant issued by a Karitzu circuit judge, and I have it swept for bugs twice a day anyway—there are some downright unscrupulous corps out there. Without privacy, I wouldn't be able to get *anything* done."

The door was right behind me, I could still make a break for it. I caught myself thinking how strange it would look if I just ran out of the house, but how it looked could be the least of my problems. I might well have made a mistake, coming to Linus'—of course I knew that. But he was the only person I knew who could give me an answer. If the price was getting caught, I was willing to pay it.

"You know, colleague, you've been acting very strangely as of late," said Linus, putting on his half-frame spectacles. "I know the bombing affected you more than you let on. That's fine, but the truth is I've been worried since well before that. You've rarely been paranoid enough to be an effective colleague. But now I must say you're more than making up for your former deficiency. You're too paranoid to function. What is all this business about?"

He knows. They called him in case I show up here. He won't give you an answer, just run.

"I'm not paying you to ask questions," I said.

"Quite right," said Linus, glaring at me over the bridge of his glasses. He thrust out an arm, exposing his watch, and then gracefully brought it within his sight. "One hour, a thousand caps," he said. "But after that, you *will* give me some answers. My study is upstairs."

We climbed a narrow staircase to a very small wood-paneled attic study. A cot rested below the window, and a chair and a small desk with a terminal sat in a corner behind the door. The two of us barely had any room to stand. Linus handed me a towel and began examining the pages.

"Well, these are trades. This is a log from the Ackerman floor, stocks, futures, bonds, equities. Looks like they took place a couple of weeks ago. What am I looking for?"

"Anything out of place?"

"I could look through these for six hours and not find even a single problem. You need to tell me what I'm looking for."

"I'm looking for trades between Ackerman colleagues— from one division to another, then back again. They call it phantom trading. I want to know if people are making fake trades to inflate income reports."

"I know what a phantom trade is. Ghosting—it crops up every now and then, but the traders usually get caught. It's a serious crime."

"I need you to see if there's any going on. Check all of these trades."

"I work in arbitrage, Charles. I know most of these traders. I can speak for the integrity of the division."

"Check it anyway."

"Okay," he said reluctantly.

I toweled off as Linus broke out a red pen and a calculator. He sat at an old-fashioned writer's desk and began reviewing the trades. He circled numbers, broke them down, put them back together in new ways, tallied and split them again. He coaxed trades, one into another, across locations and traders. When he was done he took off his spectacles.

"I've got to tell you, I don't see anything here."

My heart sank. I took a long, deep breath, the first since I fled Ackerman earlier that afternoon, the last I would have as a free man.

It was okay now. They could catch me. In fact, they already had caught me—long ago. They caught me when I did... well, whatever it was that I did to get their attention. I was fine with it, I really was. At least I knew the truth, and I was tired of running, tired of being the mouse in the maze.

And really, what had I been expecting? Either Linus would find phantom trading or not. One meant the entire world was coming to an end, the other meant only mine was. I was nauseous just trying to figure out which option I preferred.

I sat back on the bed.

"You don't look well, colleague. I can loan you some alcohol, if you would like. Maybe you need one of your sedatives?"

"I quit," I said, putting my arms behind my head.

"Oh, well that explains it. That and the cigarettes? You can't just up and quit those things. You need to do it under the supervision of a professional."

"No. I just needed to find the trades. I needed them to be there, that's all."

"Well, this is just a small sample of trading. I couldn't certify that there weren't a few traders ghosting."

"No. What I was looking for was systemic. Are you sure that all of these trades are good?"

"Well, you'd need a forensic accountant to be a hundred percent sure, but if there's ghosting going on, it's not on these pages. If it is, someone's found a new way to hide it. None of the products traded here had reciprocal trades back, in whole or in part, and most are to other corps in the Karitzu. Some pages are damaged, I can't attest to what's on those, but if you bought insider information on some kind of systemic problem, you may need to ask for your money back."

"No, that wasn't it."

"Well, I can't imagine why you wanted to find phantoms. But for what it's worth, I'm sorry. Perhaps you have other trades I could look at?"

"No," I said, defeated. "If they were there, you'd have found them right away."

"They really couldn't have been there, Charles, I'm sorry. People, new traders in particular, sometimes think that Phantom trading is a good idea. They try it, the market corrects, and they get wiped out. Getting away with corruption on a mass scale like what you seem to be describing—it's nearly impossible. Free, fair systems always win out. The invisible hand...."

I tossed the towel onto the bed.

"I know," I said. "I should have always known..."

"I can look again tomorrow, if you like. I can access all of this material from work, you don't need to print it out."

"No."

"As you like. Now there is the matter of the thousand caps?"

I nodded and leaned back on the bed. He was going to have a hell of a time getting paid. I could only be turned into so much soap.

Lightning struck, and the lights dimmed for a moment. Linus looked out the window.

"You know what, I'll run a tab. This will be a bad storm. I have some kerosene, and I think we'll need it. I'll make up a room for you and we'll settle up in the morning."

My shoulders slumped, and the tension in my body melted away. I wouldn't need to run anymore. I was caught. I could tell Linus the truth. Then at least he'd get a little money for turning me in. I could make a break for LowSec, I figured, but what would be the point? Kate was all I cared about down there. With her, I could live there forever, happy. Without her, without a contract, and with Ackerman chasing me—I could run, but I'd only die tired.

Everything she had said was a lie. Kate was fake, the Republic a fake too. *Christ*, I said to myself, *with my luck it wasn't even a conspiracy. Aisling was just some stupid lady who stole water, I got myself all worked up over it, and they nabbed me. End of story.*

I had wanted the world to end. What kind of person wishes for that?

Just then the doorbell rang. I jumped out of the bed and hit my head on the sloped ceiling.

"Christ, relax!" cried Linus. "My god, it's probably my friends. I rent them every night. I didn't bother canceling them because I didn't think that they'd show up on a night like this. They're dedicated, I'll give them that. If they ask for hazard pay, though…."

"Send them home," I said. "Send them home!"

"All right, but then you're going to tell me what's going on. I've been more than patient. I want to help, but you need to tell me everything. No more secrets, you understand me?"

I nodded, and my colleague went downstairs.

I sat there a fully rationalized, constructed criminal. Retention had invested a lot of time and money, turning me from a lonely divorcee who had gotten caught up in a young woman's silly rhetoric into a full-blown citizen.

I casually wondered if I could find any hope in Linus. He clearly had designs on me—something he had been grooming me for. He had been far too patient for what I was paying him. I could ask him for a favor—forever in his debt to save my life. I'd be a slave, but I'd live. But buying off my debt would cost him a pretty penny, and there are easier ways to get a slave. I couldn't imagine anyone would consider me a bargain at any price.

I heard muffled voices coming from downstairs. I looked at the disintegrated mass of pulp and ink into which I had poured all my hope for redemption. I had risked everything to learn that they were worthless.

The phantoms are real.

There it was. Blind optimism, false hope. I was tired of it. I had been right, Sarah Aisling did spread hope like a disease, and I was now a plague-ravished corpse. So many people had spent so much time trying to straighten me out. Linus, Corbett, even Bernard. They had faith in me as a colleague, and I had thought I knew better.

Hope is the enemy of life.

The phantoms are there. Look for them, they're there!

Hope is the antithesis of reality. If they had been there, Linus would have found them. He had spent his life in arbitrage, first as a trader, then as a manager with nearly a dozen traders under him. Nobody knew the system better.

Nobody knows the system better...

I looked one last time at the pulpy mess—no longer legible to anyone.

Corporatism breeds paranoia.

All at once I knew the truth. The pages were real. Kate was real. The crash was real and so was the Republic.

Coming to Linus had been a bigger mistake than I could have possibly imagined. He had every reason to cover it up any fraud. No one was better at this kind of thing than Linus, the man who never told the same lie twice.

And that would be the police at the door.

I jumped onto the bed and scrambled to the window. I opened it and a wild wind blew through the room. I could hear a clamor at the stairs as I climbed onto the roof, steadying myself against the wet shingles. I became aware of my injuries, my ankle and my knee giving in to utter exhaustion. I had nothing left, no tension in the muscles. But I couldn't quit. Not until I knew for sure.

The branches of a giant oak tree were swaying violently alongside the house. One branch was close enough for me to reach. It wouldn't support my full weight, but it steadied me enough that I could reach the edge of the roof, where I might be able to jump onto a major limb.

I couldn't make out any of the shouting behind me, but I didn't dare look back. I took a deep breath and jumped. I only half landed on the branch, my arms barely over it. I slipped on the wet, naked skin of the oak, clawing to get up. When that didn't work, I tried just to keep from falling. But my strength failed, and I tumbled down onto the soft earth below.

I wanted to lie there. I wasn't a death-sport athlete, I had no training for this kind of physical exertion, and my body rebelled against the latest blow. All of the air had left my lungs, and my muscles fought against any attempt to use them.

I rolled over and then climbed onto my hands and knees. Parked behind Linus' car was a police cruiser, the headlights still shining onto his front door.

They had left the engine running.

I stumbled to my feet and hobbled to the car. I heard the crackle of electricity as an ionized taser bolt fell from the attic window. Two more crashed around me, but I was able to reach the car. As I did, Linus and another officer came out the front door. The officer pulled out his tasegun. I opened the driver door and ducked down. Bolts flew over my head. I jumped inside as more blasts ricocheted harmlessly off the windshield.

I threw the car into reverse and slammed the pedal to the floor. A horrendous squeal came from the tires as they spun in place, screaming over the wet pavement. The officer made a dash for the car. I tried again, slower this time, and the wheels found traction. The cruiser began pulling out into the street, but the cop caught up. He jumped onto the hood of the car and pulled out his baton. I hit the gas, driving backward down the street. He grabbed the rim of the hood and held on as I tried to shake him. Crashing through a fence and over several bushes, I finally found an open space.

I turned the wheel as far as I could. The car spun a donut, and the officer was flung off. I threw the car into drive and crashed back into the street, where Linus and the other officer were running toward me. I turned the other way, accelerating off into the darkness—farther into the storm.

18

My hands were shaking so violently that I struggled to keep the wheel straight. I punched on the siren so I could skirt whatever little traffic was on the streets.

Heading toward the city wall, I could already see neighborhoods without power. I would have to flee the city fast and then find shelter somewhere.

No doubt Linus had already been pushing the officers to call their precinct and report the vehicle stolen. But the cruiser was an expensive car, and they wouldn't call it in before they cobbled together an excuse (something in which they resisted valiantly as I, the great gun-wielding, martial arts grandmaster Charles Thatcher, sneak-attacked them under cover of night, robbing them of their keys and car).

I drove as fast as I could for the city gates. They saw the police lights well before I arrived, and opened up an emergency lane for me. I chuckled as I imagined the list of fines racking up against me: impersonating a cop, obstruction of traffic, theft of corporate property, assault, identity theft. And that was all since this morning. Was there an upper limit—a record for the most number of infractions incurred in one day? I wondered if I should total the car, just for sport.

Once I passed into LowSec, it was nearly impossible to see. I used the cruiser's radar and infrared, but there was no power anywhere. The streetlights, the homes, they were all dark. I traveled no more than a few miles before the remote kill switch kicked in. The car choked, sputtered out, and rolled to a stop.

I sat there, my hands on the wheel, the roar of a hurricane now at full strength just outside the four doors of the disabled vehicle. I wanted to stay inside it, ride out the storm. But even in LowSec, in the middle of a hurricane, they'd find a stolen cruiser.

As I opened the door, I was overwhelmed by an intense desire to commit one last protest, to do them one final outrage.

The car was locked up—I couldn't roll it into a ditch, and it was too heavy for me to flip over. I opened the trunk, but I couldn't find any kerosene or the like with which to burn or blow it up. I found a shotgun, which might have done the trick, but it was locked up.

I went back to the driver's side and wrenched the sun visor from the roof. I threw it to the ground and repeatedly stomped on it. Then I ran triumphantly into the night.

I should have stayed as far away from Kate's apartment as I could. But I had, thus far, done a fabulous job of avoiding the smart thing to do, and had no intention of blemishing that record. Besides, I had no money, no contract, no friends, and what was no doubt a substantial price on my head. Without help I'd be lucky to last more than a day or two in LowSec, and starving to death in the gutter wasn't any better than rotting in jail or facing the noose.

Darting back and forth between the buildings, in and out of shuttered warehouses and broken-down apartments, I felt my strength coming back to me. Maybe I was excited about the possibly finding an answer, or just being outside of Capital City, but what was a four-hour hike through the back streets of LowCon felt like a few minutes.

With luck I'd find an empty apartment, and Kate would already be in the bunker. I could then, at the very least, say that someone had survived this devilry.

Her neighborhood was dark. The power was out, and only a few apartments were using candles or kerosene lamps. The warehouse was in rough shape. It was abandoned, one corner of the aluminum roof completely torn off. Someone had gone through a good deal of trouble to lock all of the doors, so I went in through one of the windows.

Water was pouring in from every crevice—down all the pipes and cement pillars. The drums, bookshelves and bedsprings all remained, but the fires had long gone out and anything of value had been taken. I knelt down, and with each lightning strike I looked for evidence of a fight: blood, bullet holes or shell casings.

A small stream of water was flowing down the back steps, as if someone had left all the faucets on. I ran up three flights to the roof. It was cracked and rusted out, with large gashes and missing aluminum plates. I worked my way slowly to the southwest corner, sometimes getting on my hands and knees to crawl over particularly slippery or damaged spots.

From the corner I was able to get a good look at Kate's apartment building. The hallways were lit only by emergency lighting, and I was surprised even by that. One or two of the apartments were lit by kerosene, but other than that there was no sign of life. I looked at the other buildings, marking their location and then scanning quickly with each strike of lightning. But I spied no snipers, no police cruisers, no evidence at all that Ackerman was there.

I waited an hour, both out of an abundance of caution and the growing realization that I'd have to find my way back down. What had seemed like a good idea under the threat of an Ackerman ambush now struck me as a terrible mistake. My adrenaline spent, I wondered how I had even managed to get across. A single slip or weakness in the roof, and I'd fall three stories onto a concrete floor. I wondered if I could fashion a rope out of my clothing and climb down, but the idea was ludicrous. I was terrified to go back the way I came, but, wet and shivering, I couldn't survive huddled in the corner much longer.

After a few minutes I remembered the fire escape on the southern wall. It was rusted out and didn't reach the roof, so I had forgotten all about it. But maybe I could jump down to it.

I discovered a twelve-foot drop onto the top platform. I held my breath and leapt. As I landed, it wrenched itself from the wall. It spun around and, by some miracle, dumped me onto the level below before landing on top of me in a heap.

I felt along the wet bars of my prison, trying to get a sense of its geometry. A railing lay on top of me, and the platform had split, caging me in. But I came upon a gap in the entanglement, and slowly I worked my way through. I found the steps and climbed down to the final landing. I lowered the emergency ladder and took it down to the street.

The roar of the storm had gotten so loud that I wouldn't have been able to hear myself scream. I crossed the street to her building as stealthily as I could. The front door was locked. I worked my way into the back alley, over the mounds of trash, and to a hallway window. I smashed it and climbed in.

The emergency lights had grown dim, and were beginning to flicker. A crying baby reassured me that there was at least some life in this building.

When I reached her apartment I found the front door slightly ajar. I examined the frame and the lock, but I didn't spot any sign that the door had been forced. I put my back to the wall, opened the door, and then looked around the corner.

Lightning lit up the room. In that brief moment it looked completely empty, the couch, the pots and pans, the chairs— all gone.

I took several deep breaths and slid into the apartment. The kitchen counter seemed bare. I ran my hands over it; the can of tallow, herbs and infuser were all gone. I opened a drawer and ran my hand inside, but it was empty.

Then I noticed a large, dark object on the far end of the living room. Hard to make out, it loomed by the far wall near the bathroom. Whatever it was, it didn't belong.

I took a step toward it. My heart quickened. I was sure now; there was something in the room with me.

I saw the glow of a cigar and could almost hear the deep inhalation. In the brief blue light of another flash of lightning, I saw a large, overstuffed red leather chair, and a man in a dark suit sitting in it.

"Hello, Mr. Thatcher," he said. I hadn't heard a human voice in six hours; it cut through the air louder than any thunder.

I couldn't breathe, or run, or move. For a moment, like a child, I had the silly notion that he hadn't actually seen me, that he just guessed that I was there and if I didn't move he'd dismiss me. But in the next flash I could tell—he was looking straight at me.

"Who are you?" I whispered.

"You know who I am," he said.

It had been a mistake to come. My mind rushed through escape routes, trying to think of a way to undo this catastrophic mistake. But all I could do was hope that I would wake up from this nightmare. Instead, I found relief in the form of a sudden blow to the back of my head.

19

I woke up to find myself in the most comfortable bed I had ever slept in. I thought that I must have died, and through some miracle of nature (or an accounting debacle at the pearly gates) found myself in heaven. Then I realized I was in prison.

The bedroom itself was only a touch smaller than my entire apartment. Everything was white—the walls, the bed, and the carpeting. The room looked brand-new, as if I was the first person to occupy it. The mattress was soft; the duvet seemed to be genuine goose down—more expensive per ounce than gold. I ran my hand down the length of the sheets until I found the label—cotton, twelve-hundred thread count. My pajamas were silk, and fit like they were custom tailored for me.

It was the closest you could actually get to returning to the womb. Even Linus didn't sleep this well.

Yep, this was prison.

HighCons got all the bad prison cells—rats, concrete beds and iron bars—in a room made of cinder blocks with four other people and a single toilet. It was a preview of what life would be like if you didn't cooperate. LowCons were treated the exact opposite, given a private suite to rival the most luxurious hotels, so that you could understand the true benevolence of your Corporation, and to stoke your desire for the finer things. Prison gave the higher grades something to fear, and the lower grades something to envy. This wasn't a cell, it was psychological warfare.

One entire wall was glass. I opened the curtains and looked out onto a triangular atrium some twenty-three floors below me. I knew immediately where I was—the Retention Division Prison Complex, the Citadel, a three-sided building in Ackerman's northernmost territory.

Hundreds of cells filled the two walls opposite mine, going up at least another twenty floors to a huge skylight above. The sun was out, and it looked as if the sky here never darkened. Far below me was a park, though whether it was for inmates or staff I couldn't tell. The distance across the atrium was too far for me to make out faces in the cells across from me, but I noticed other people looking out into the courtyard, all wearing the same white pajamas.

I ignored my slippers, walking barefoot into the living room. It had a sunken, hardwood floor, with a large sofa, a beautiful comfort chair, and a forty-two-inch television. There was a bar, a kitchen, and a coffee table with fresh fruit on it.

I wonder if this is the room they put Malcolm Evans in.

On the far side of the room was a sliding door. I walked over to it, and much to my surprise it whooshed open. Two men in butler's uniforms stood in a hallway on the other side, one with a fine white cloth draped over his arm.

"Oh," I stammered, disappointed that they had so easily caught me testing the bounds of my cell.

"Mr. Thatcher," said the shorter one, "you're up. How did you sleep?"

"Fine."

"I'm pleased to hear it. Your injuries have been tended. How do you feel?"

"Good," I said. "I feel good."

"I can get the doctor for you. Would you like a follow-up examination?"

"No, really, I'm fine."

"That's wonderful news. You were out quite a long time, you must be hungry. Can I get you something?"

"Oh. No, thank you."

"Honestly sir," said the man, a broad smile across his face, "it would be my pleasure to get you something you'd enjoy. What would you like? Please?"

I shook my head.

"You know, Mr. Thatcher, some guests do have trouble adjusting—it's completely normal. But I assure you, everything here is for your benefit. It's all free."

"Are you joking?" I croaked.

"No, of course not sir. With our compliments. Don't worry about money at all during your stay with us, you won't be charged a thing. Now about that meal?"

"Oh, I have some fruit and I'll bet the fridge is stocked," I said. "Don't worry about it."

"Don't be silly, Mr. Thatcher. I believe the kitchen may have closed, but tell me what you'd like, and I'll see if I can get them to whip it up for you."

It was a trap, it had to be. The psychological warfare had begun. I was curious to see what they would do if I actually ordered something.

"What is on the menu?"

"It would be far easier for you to ask for something. If we can't make it, I'll let you know, but I think you'll be surprised. We have an extensive kitchen. Please, I *challenge* you to come up with something we can't do," he said.

"I... well, are you sure?"

"The challenge stands, sir. What's your pleasure?"

I did need to eat. I tried to think of an esoteric meal, something with real meat, something my captors couldn't possibly have.

"There is one thing, an old fashioned kind of sandwich, I'm not sure if you've ever heard of it. A Reuben? Can you make one of those?"

"Of course, sir, excellent choice! Rye bread, I assume? I don't take you for one of those who would sully such a sandwich on white?"

"No. No. Rye, I guess. Of course."

"Very good, Mr. Thatcher."

"Please, call me Charles," I said, now uncomfortable.

"Of course, sir," he replied.

"You don't need to say 'sir.' You can just say Charles."

"Of course, Mr. Thatcher."

I rubbed the bridge of my nose. "You are not going to call me Charles, are you?"

"I'm afraid not, sir. We are prohibited."

"Couldn't you have just said so?"

"Oh, my goodness no, sir. It would be terribly rude to contradict you." The man bowed again and went on his task, leaving the other man behind.

I continued exploring my cell. I found a small private gym with a slender pool, a jet contrived such that you could swim endlessly against the current. A treadmill, a host of free weights, and an exercise bike were all waiting to be used. I even uncovered a small library, about the size of a walk-in closet.

The library intrigued me. I had never had time to read for pleasure, and most people found it rather snobbish anyway. The shelves hosted books on nearly every subject, even ones I had scarcely heard of—long dead Eastern and Western philosophies, like Buddhism and Christianity—as well as the usual litany of books written by CEOs on the importance of greed and loyalty.

There was a bounty of delights for me to indulge in, and I had just scratched the surface. But the simple act of ordering a sandwich had already made me feel guilty. People in LowSec were starving, and I was getting a sandwich with real meat. That, in their eyes, was why I was broken.

Then I spotted an original copy of the Zinov'yevna Bible. I hadn't looked at it in years, and while I quoted it often, I hadn't actually read it fully through. It wasn't a bible, in the conventional sense, but an epic fairy tale, a story about a group of capitalists who remake the world into a utopian free market. I opened it to a random page and began reading:

People think that a liar gains a victory over his victim. What I've learned is that a lie is an act of self-abdication, because one surrenders one's reality to the person to whom one lies, making that person one's master, condemning oneself from then on to faking the sort of reality that person's view requires to be faked. And if one gains the immediate purpose of the lie—the price one pays is the destruction of what the gain was intended to serve.

Was that Zino's Objective reality? The biggest complaint I ever heard against socialism was that it was idealistic—that it didn't take the selfish nature of man into account, that people would game the system. But here was Zinov'yevna saying things as idealistic, unrealistic, and unhinged from reality as anything said by Karl Marx. Kate was right; the capitalists in the bible were all gentlemen. None of them lied or took advantage of their superior positions. When has a person ever been like that except in a work of fiction?

But maybe Zino was right. Maybe all lies did come back to destroy the liar. Maybe that was why we were all going to come to such a terrible end. But that never seemed to stop the lies, never seemed to stop the violence.

I had seen people suffer their own lies. But I had never seen anything so magnificent as to suggest that no one who lied had ever profited from it. And certainly when they lied, they didn't just injure themselves. More often than not, the innocent suffered lies at least as much the guilty.

The engine of the economy ran on lies, and those who profited the most were those who learned not to get caught.

Zino believed in unbridled competition. But how could that be any less extreme, idyllic or naïve than the thought of sharing all the wealth? We called socialists "plunderers". But if capitalism proved anything, it was that those who loot and plunder don't need socialism to do it.

If all people were as gentlemanly, honest, and honorable as Zino's capitalists, socialism would have worked too.

I put the book back in its place and surveyed my cell. If you truly wanted competition, if you wanted the best to rise to the top—you needed everybody to start at the same place—no handouts or legs up, earn only by the sweat of your brow. But I never saw a HighCon so committed to that principle that he'd deny his family the advantages of wealth, let his family get the same education, healthcare, and police protection as everyone else.

No, Kate was right. HighCons were hypocrites who lectured on the Moral Hazard of giving people things they didn't earn, while taking for themselves every advantage handed to them.

How could a LowCon compete against people who had private gyms, libraries, servants? A HighCon would tell you that he deserved these rewards and ridicule LowCons for failing to compete. But the game was rigged against them.

And when a LowCon was so rude as to point this out, to ask for fair treatment and access to essential services, HighCons complained, argued about class warfare and that people were trying to take what was rightfully theirs—rightfully inherited, rightfully stolen, or rightfully leveraged off the sweat of LowCons. Corporations demanded that governments take their thumbs off the scale—remove the regulation—so that they put their own thumbs on. They would hold up the few rare exceptions (which could be counted on one hand)—the LowCons who had risen through the ranks all the way to executive—and say "See, it can be done," as if the poor who were kicked out of their homes or starved to death simply didn't want it badly enough.

The few generous people I had ever heard of, those who actually built companies, employed people, and put money back into the system, the ones HighCons point to when people accused them of pillaging, were almost always the ones who started poor. Those born into wealth thought they deserved it and made money destroying. Those born poor who became rich from their own ingenuity and hard work were the ones most likely to be charitable. If the system was right, why would those very examples of the success of that system– those who truly earned it themselves—be generous? The people who had lived on both sides of the economic spectrum, who had the best perspective from which to judge, most bemoaned the terrible inequalities against LowCons.

The butler arrived with my sandwich. It smelled divine, made from real meat, a delicacy in a world with such little space for livestock. But I couldn't eat it. I opened the refrigerator and looked for the least expensive thing I could find, but it was filled with fruits and cheeses.

In the living room I found a small velvet box sitting on top of the television. It was a poker set. The dice were made of tiger bone, the shooters elephant tusk. The entire set was easily worth more than the sum total of the staff and equipment of the whole seventh floor where I worked.

I turned on the television. It had (of course) every channel I had ever heard of, and many I hadn't. Some charged as much as three hundred caps a minute. I laughed, turned it to the CEO channel and left it running.

Let them bill me for this. I'm not getting out of here alive anyway.

A seminar popped onto the screen, a CEO giving a lecture on management.

"The second postulate is 'Perception is everything,'" he said. "Reality isn't important, and you have no control over it, so there's no point in worrying about it. Even caps aren't real. They're paper, bits of electrons stored electronically. You cannot eat them or live in them. The only value they have is what you can trade for them, and you can only trade what someone else *thinks* they're worth. Convince someone that they're worth less, and you earn more caps from sales; convince someone that they're worth more, and you spend fewer on purchases. It's all perception.

"Every year perfectly sound banks are destroyed because someone starts a rumor that the bank is unstable. This causes a run on the bank, which then loses capital. This, of course, makes it unstable. The perception actually creates the reality. Manage perception, and you create reality."

I went back to the library. I looked for Nash, but couldn't find him, though I did find more than one copy of *The Origin of Species*.

I was leafing through the books when I noticed a small cabinet down at the bottom. I opened it to find a ream of paper and a small typewriter. It was old and worn, so much so that it hardly looked like it belonged.

What on earth is this here for? I wondered. Had they left it there by accident? Did they want me to write something? If I did, they'd almost surely destroy it, or use it against me in court. Still, I was going to be there for weeks, maybe months. I'd need something to do. I made a note of it and returned it to its place.

"The third postulate," continued the voice on the screen, "is 'Fire ten percent of your workforce every year.' This makes your corporation leaner and more efficient. You should be hiring about that much anyway, so you shouldn't shrink much. But the fear this instills, the drive to compete, is invaluable. Also you'll be bringing in fresh blood, which can help you find the newest bright stars—colleagues with executive potential. You'll also save money, since even at the same grade, the new contracts will start at a lower rank. The real problem will be people who have been in the corporation the longest, the ones who you pay the most. Consider finding ways of replacing them with lower-rank, less expensive colleagues.

"Now, it's become common for employees—especially those represented by advocates—to protect against this by working tenure clauses into their contracts. Avoid hiring these troublemakers when you can. But if you really need the talent, remember that you can always fire for cause, which is, of course, just another matter of perception. If the employee doesn't like it, he can always litigate. But the first one to litigate, you destroy; bury him with motions, cross-motions, and injunctions. The process is expensive, but do it once and you'll never have to do it again."

I opened the cabinets in the kitchen and found loads of dishes: complete sets of silverware, place settings, wine glasses and serving trays. I checked the sofa. Sure enough, it was a foldout.

Guests? Are they expecting I'll entertain?

"The fourth postulate is to always keep things moving. Never let the company stagnate. Every eight to sixteen months you should come up with a new division, a new paradigm, or a new mission statement. Pick a new product that you can tell people will be the next big thing. Much of being a CEO is paying people to dig ditches so that you can pay other people to fill them in again. Busy people are easier to control. Corporations are in a constant state of decay. You have to continuously re-organize to keep your people occupied."

I laughed.

"The fifth postulate is 'Always lie.' Lie about everything. If your stock is doing well, say that you don't like how it's going; you'll be lauded for your ambition. If the stock is bad, admitting it makes it worse, so say you're pleased with it. Figure out how it could've been worse and focus on that. And for God's sake, never tell the same lie twice. It's lazy, and it's how you get caught. If paychecks were late last week because of a worker's strike, next week they should be late because of an accounting error."

This must be the channel that Linus watches.

"If you're telling the truth about anything," he continued, "you're missing an opportunity to leverage. Information is power, and if you're going to give accurate information, make people pay through the nose for it. The truth is a commodity; manage your stock of it."

I fell onto the orchid-white couch. For a moment I worried that I might stink it up, but that wasn't my problem. Still, I felt my face, and realized I could use a shower and shave. I was loath to avail myself of any of these luxuries. Besides, maybe meeting my interrogators smelling like a rotting pig was its own rebellion. But I wanted to face them with my head held high, with pride.

I hopped into the shower. The water was warm, clean, and decalcified. The soap melted away all my dirt and left me smelling fresh. I hadn't realized until then just what a good shower did, and I stood there for fifteen minutes, doing nothing but letting the water run over my aching body.

I realized that could probably even drink the water. I wondered if maybe my life had been harder on me than I had ever understood.

I could feel myself rejuvenated, ready to face whatever they threw at me. Now was the time to collect myself, to formulate a plan of attack.

They would interrogate me. They would know about Kate, and maybe about the Republic. I'd have to steel myself against attacks on that front. She might have already been captured, but I had to hold out hope. If she had been real, she'd need my help. Against torture, nobody can hold out forever. But I'd hold out long enough.

They'll offer you your life back—a bump in grade. Make them think you'll take it, let them keep offering more and more. But never, ever take it, no matter what! Let them come, in the end, to see that I have no price.

I would have to begin enjoying myself, I thought. I must make it look like they have me, like I'll bow to their demands. I would eat their food, read their books, use their gym and watch their television.

I lathered up a second time, grinning, ready to fight.

But what if that was what they wanted? Was that how they'd break me? Maybe they wouldn't offer me anything; maybe they already had Kate, and destroyed the Republic. If they needed me to get her, would they have waited so long to begin my interrogation? Certainly they were as aware as I was that every minute helped her and her friends get away.

I thought desperately on how to foil these people, to ruin their plans, whatever they were. Whatever they wanted of me, I needed to do the opposite. If they wanted me sad, I would be happy. If they wanted me to suffer, I would relish. Defiant, I would bend.

But I had no idea what they wanted. I didn't even know if the Republic had been real or not, let alone if they'd ask me about it.

At that moment I knew that they had me right where they wanted me.

20

The guards came for me later that evening. They gave me modest encouragement, told me not to worry. After years of working there, they said, they could spot the ones who would make it and the ones who wouldn't. I had a real chance—Ackerman wouldn't let Retention destroy a valuable asset.

"Cheer up! You're corporate material!"

We wound through the hallways till we got to a beautiful glass elevator overlooking the atrium. It dropped down all twenty-three floors, through the ground floor and down another dozen or so, to an underground labyrinth of rooms. They took me down a white hallway, past rows of sliding doors. Finally we got to one at the end, and they stopped.

"Whatever happens, Mr. Thatcher," the guard said, "keep your chin up!"

Stepping through the door was like stepping into another world. There was a small foyer with a red wooden bench. Chinese scrolls hung from the ceiling, and beads hung in the doorway. The main room was oriental (at least how the oriental designs appeared in books—most of those lands had long since flooded). Red, gold and black paintings and icons hung everywhere. Cherry and ebony tiger, dragon, and warrior figurines were on nearly every conceivable surface. An ancient Chinese writing desk squatted against the corner of the wall, and two large silver dragons lined the adjoining sides of the room, with several lacquered screens in the corners. Atop the writing desk I saw a small wooden case, gilded and adorned in black enamel. I knew immediately what it was: a poker set.

If the contents of my room were worth more than the entire seventh floor, this room was worth more than the entire building.

Never in my life, in my wildest dreams, had I thought that such power existed.

"Hello, Charles."

One of the small screens obscured a thin hallway, from which came an executive. He was the man I had met in Kate's apartment. He wore a black suit with a golden tie, and was so well groomed and preened that even Linus would have looked disheveled by comparison. It was as if the man had been born an adult, in his suit, and he wore it like armor, like he was bulletproof.

I could make out his features much better than the last time I saw him. His skin was a burnt bronze, his hair a dirty blond, and he had a very thin beard, like stubble, but shaved in deliberate, sharp lines at his cheeks and neck.

He walked past me to the writing desk, where he opened a hidden recess in the back and withdrew a bottle of whiskey.

I wondered how many other hidden compartments this place had, and what else they held.

"I understand you drink whiskey?" he said.

He motioned to the sofa and invited me to take a seat. Two glasses were already set out on the small table. The executive poured some of the golden liquid into only one. He re-corked the bottle before concealing it back in its original place.

"Do you know why you are here?"

"You're going to torture me."

He laughed.

"What a barbaric mind you have, my friend. No, you will not be tortured. You are here because you are broken. You are a complex machine, which for some reason doesn't run right. You can't even perform rudimentary tasks properly. You are here to be rehabilitated."

"Rehabilitated?" I mused. We both knew that my fate was already decided.

"Of course. Nobody is mad at you or wants revenge; that would be immoral. If you can be repaired, returned to some level of usefulness to the corporation, we'd like to see that. You have a massive debt to pay off, and you could do a better job of that if we fixed you rather than if we simply sold your organs off for scrap. We're not barbarians."

He raised the glass and held it. "This," he said, "is called scotch. It used to be very popular, but it came only from Scotland. They called this particular kind a 'peat'; it came only from the southern swamps. They've been frozen solid for centuries. Even if the world were restored back to its original climate, the swamps will never come back. Another bottle of this will never be made by man," he said, taking a large gulp.

I looked at my own glass, which he had failed to fill.

"Oh. Well, I would like very much to offer you some, but your palate is nowhere near refined enough to taste the difference between this and goat urine. It would be a shameful waste—quite literally a crime—to share this with you. I have too much respect for the company, without whose profits I could not have purchased this, to do that. Respect, Charles."

I laughed.

"What's so funny? Please, contrary to popular belief, I am always eager to hear a good joke."

"You act as if you are so much better than me, but you're not. You're not, and we both know it. Do you think I'm impressed by your scotch?"

"Oh my, you misunderstand," the executive said, his arms moving in broad strokes. "No, no, no, I'm not trying to impress you, by no means. I make in a single day what you make in a year. Since this conversation started I have already earned more than you will ever have. I would be a pretty shallow man indeed if, in spite of all that, I cared at all about your opinion," he said, taking another sip.

"Say what you will," I answered. "You care. You're a joke, showing off with your material wealth, trying to intimidate me, show me how successful you are."

"Dear, dear, dear. You know, I've heard it said that executives have very big egos, that we think the world revolves around us. Well, Charles, what would they say about you, sitting there, thinking that I would be moved by your opinion of me?"

"You don't even need these things," I said. "Look at you, all of your money, your oriental rugs, your poker set, and your elaborate ornaments. You buy these things so you can feel important."

"Goodness gracious," the man said, gently putting his hand into his coat pocket. "Is that what you think? My friend, I don't spend money because I want to. Far from it. I do it because it is my responsibility, because it is the moral thing to do."

He pulled a cigar from his pocket, snipped the end, and put it in his mouth. "The economy can only function so long as we consume. Money is made to be spent. Just sitting there it's worthless. When I buy things, I improve the lives of those below me. Why, I redesign this office at least twice a year just to keep people employed. And the people I employ, like good colleagues, spend the money that *they* earn. That money inexorably, albeit regrettably, even makes its way to people like you. I have built entire micro-economies with my spending, and kept many a colleague out of the gutter. That is respect, Charles. That is love."

"Yeah, you spend the money on yourself, showing off or giving it to your friends and family."

He lit the cigar and puffed a few times to get a good burn going. I took the opportunity to look at the swords, ancient blunderbusses, pistols, and other decorations on the walls.

I wondered if they were real. I could snatch one maybe, but I doubted I'd make it past the elevator. Still, running him through with his own sword might have been its own reward.

"I give money to no one, Charles. Giving is for communists. I do, naturally, have a savings, which I use to ensure my children get low-interest loans and stipends for their educations, help them become high-contracts. But I do this because they come from me, I raised them, and I know the corporation and its colleagues will benefit from their success. I can trust them with money far more than I could trust a stranger, more than I could trust you. My god, what would you do if you ever earned any *real* money? Keep it? That's awfully selfish of you, don't you think?"

"I'd use it to help those who need it."

"That's what I do," he said.

"No, no, I'd give it to them. I'd help them directly!"

"Precisely why you can't be trusted with money." he said, stabbing the air with the smoldering cigar. "The poor cannot handle money, that's why they're poor. Give a poor man ten caps, and he won't use that money to invest in the future, or to buy a ride to a job interview, or to get a book and read it. No, he will buy a bottle of potato vodka and be done with it. You've done him a terrible disservice. Now he's lost self-respect, and he's learned that he doesn't need to earn money, that all he has to do is be poor and people will pay him. It's a vicious cycle, and every day he'll act even more pitiable to earn even more charity.

"If, however, you had taken that ten caps and purchased something, if others like you did the same, then a factory would be built, and that man can be put to work. Oh, I believe you, my friend. I believe you'd show charity. That's why you can't be trusted.

"The truth is that you're selfish. You and your kind would drive our society to ruin out of a conceited desire to convince others of your altruistic nature. You're the one trying to impress people. You talk about charity, taxes, a greater good, and about a social compact, because deep down you're terrified of your own failures, because if you don't convince people to take their eyes off of competition they might just see you for the failure that you are, Charles. And if they see that, and you haven't convinced them of the importance of charity, where will you be?"

"But you don't have to give the poor money. You can create social programs—"

"Ahhh," he said, taking a deep drag from the cigar. "The leviathan…"

"Government, it's better. You know it is."

"Of course! Absolutely! Do you think I don't like the leviathan?" he said, throwing his hands up. "It's marvelous, my friend, simply marvelous. What I wouldn't give for a leviathan—take everything I own, please, take it if you can build one.

"But you can't. It's an idea, an abstraction, a fairytale. Nobody has ever gotten one to work; trying is no more productive than looking for the Easter Rabbit. The leviathan requires compassion. Compassion does not exist, Charles. It's an illusion. Even your self-declared altruism, the money you would give to others, is motivated purely out of a desire to end your own agony at watching them suffer, to alleviate your own sense of guilt. I feel guilt too. I've simply learned to use it productively. By our very nature we do what is in our own best interest—we are incapable of doing otherwise.

That is why the leviathans all failed—because they allowed, even encouraged, belief in fantasy."

"Compassion exists. I have seen it."

"It was an illusion. Have you read history?" he asked, taking another sip. He turned his back and strolled casually toward the far wall, as if daring me to grab a weapon and strike him. "Any history, it doesn't matter…" he said. "Has there ever been a time when man did not betray his fellow man? A time when man's urge to compete, to dominate, did not win out over this 'compassion' you believe in."

"It happens…"

"Only by accident, only in errors of nature—predicted by Darwin himself, mutations which fight against the natural order of things," he said, taking a moment to check the alignment of one of his paintings. "In short, Charles, only in you."

"I am not alone."

He turned back toward me. "We are all alone. We always have been, always will be. Convincing people otherwise, getting them to fight and die for the leviathan, religion, or a corporation, may have its advantage. But we are all alone. Wishing otherwise, no matter how hard you try, will not make it so."

He wants to break me. But he won't. Not in a hundred years.

"You are like a child, closing your eyes, thinking if you believe in something enough, sacrifice enough, devote yourself to it, then it must be true. You are like the religious zealot who blows himself up in the name of something he will never see or touch, convinced that the very act itself is enough to commit the reality.

"Build a society on the premise that man will not betray man and you will fail. Surely you can see that. That is why the corporation is an absolute good; it does not expect more of us than we can do. It is based on the knowledge that everyone will betray everyone else. It thrives because it lives off greed and selfishness, our most basic instincts, the ones without which we would not be the dominant species on the planet. Align yourself with that state of nature, the state of corruption—allow for it, embrace it—instead of wasting time trying to ferret it out, and you'll be a success."

"But you can't build a society based on corruption."

"And yet we have."

"But it'll fail."

"You underestimate the greed of man. The corporation is a boat far harder to sink than most people believe. In the end, no matter how bad things get, everybody wants it to survive. Everyone has a vested interest in it—from the CEO to the night janitor—and they will do anything to keep it going. The corporation is life, every one of us will defend it, no matter how corrupt it is, because it *is* us."

"No, I've seen the records. The whole system is going to collapse."

Reaching the end of his cigar, the executive went back to the writing desk and extinguished the remains in a black marble ashtray. "You've seen the records, but you don't have the intelligence to decipher them. You say the system is going to collapse only because it's what someone told you. Someone told you that Hobbes' *Leviathan* was about democracy, good works, and the social compact, and you believed that too. But they lied. Hobbes believed in the brutal tyranny and absolute power of a single ruler."

"That's not true."

"Have you read his work? I swear to you it's true."

"It's about government."

"No, Charles. Hobbes called government the leviathan—not because it was big and bloated like the sea beast—but because the ruler of mankind should be like that biblical beast, answerable only to God."

"Corporatism will end. I swear to you. If not now, then someday. Even if it takes a millennia, your 'great' system will collapse."

"Of course it will," he said sternly, turning toward me again. "I should hope it does. I believe in competition, in evolution. So I know we have the best system ever invented. But no system is static. If, in two thousand years, someone hasn't invented a better one, then man certainly doesn't deserve his place at the top of the ladder."

"But that's the point," I said. "When a corporation fails, when the system fails, the executives will walk away with all their money, and they will say they did the best they could, and that they deserve their compensation, and those who broke their backs every day for the company will get nothing. It's not fair!"

"It is the very definition of fair. It's the workers' own fault that the they walk away with nothing; they choose to. You can't blame executives for being smarter than them."

"Nobody chooses to fail."

"Of course they do. Not taking what is rightfully yours is a choice—the choice of inaction. LowCons outnumber executives a hundred to one. They could raze the entire city if they wanted, and take the money you say we owe them. But they never do. That is why they are LowCons. That is how I know they deserve to be LowCons. They choose it. And we walk away with the money because that's what we choose."

"Because they won't kill you?" I scoffed. "Because they aren't violent?"

"Exactly. Nature *is* violence. You can only survive off the death of others. Plants, animals, whatever you choose to eat, we all commit violence against other living organisms. We murder so that we may live. Violence is not pleasant, and I would not wish it on anyone, certainly not myself. But anyone who refuses to resort to violence when needed is choosing to be selected out. I did not create that system, Charles, it is nature."

"But we've evolved beyond that! That's the point of civilization, to stop the violence, to overcome that part of our nature, to be better. It's part of nature, but it's not the sum total of our human experience."

The man laughed. "Of course not. Corruption, coercion, intimidation, are all techniques to avoid violence, to create civilization."

"But that's the same thing. All of those lead to violence. The inevitable conclusion of capitalism is war!"

The man smiled broadly, like he was proud of me, and yet somehow like I had set myself up as the punch line of a perfect joke.

"Lenin said that. The First World War was commonly held to be started by the assassination of an archduke. But that was just an excuse. People are assassinated all the time. What Lenin discovered, what truly frightened him, was that the war was the result of a capitalist boom. Germany was growing, and it needed more leverage to compete with other nations and satisfy their growing economic demands. But they could no longer purchase what they needed, so they took it. Japan did the same thing decades later. Lenin was a smart man but, as communists are so apt to do, he missed the point completely."

I didn't want to give him the satisfaction of asking. But I did.

"Then what is the point?" I said.

A malevolent grin broke over his face.

"Capitalism *is* war."

I looked down at the floor.

"Man's state of nature is war, war with himself, war with all that which is around him. What you call 'civilization' is nothing more than a set of constraints used by people with power to wage war on people without it, to dominate them using the minimum possible effort.

"No war on this planet has ever been about anything other than economics, about who controls the resources to create and sustain life. Even religion is nothing more than a means of mobilizing troops to economic ends. The belief in a supreme being, when leveraged properly, is an invaluable motivator of human assets, nothing more."

"But in a state of war, you're constantly in danger. The next bombing, the next attack, a corporation might kill you."

"My god, Charles, you don't know the half of it," he laughed. "Do you think it's the thought of other corporations killing me that keeps me up at night? No, it's that one of my own colleagues will take me out. That bombing at the coffee shop last week, the one with which you are so familiar? Like a common MidCon, it never even crossed your mind that maybe the bomber wasn't from Kabul at all. Maybe the bomber was Ackerman."

I shook my head. "The reports said that he was Kabul!"

"Who wrote those reports? Perception Management, people like you, people who lie. Maybe our CEO needed an excuse to attack Kabul without violating the Karitzu's free-trade pact. We could have tricked an Epsilon into making the attack and warned the police ahead of time, let the bomber get just close enough to make a point."

"You mean—a colleague did that?"

"My god, you truly are stupid. What I'm saying is: there's no way to know. And frankly, who cares? The reality doesn't matter, only the perception. And as a loyal employee I perceive exactly what Ackerman tells me to.

"But more to the point—I'm fully aware that I'm at least as likely to die at the hands of a colleague as I am from another corp. Half my bosses want me dead, since I'm competing—quite capably, I might add—for their jobs. I make myself indispensable, which protects me, but it makes me a threat too. Being an executive is to walk a tightrope far more treacherous than any MidCon could possibly understand. I can do it only because nature has selected me to. It is a burden, of course. But it is one I carry for you, for all my colleagues, whom I love—even though you hate me for it. It's what makes me better than you, that level of selflessness."

"That's not a life."

"Well, you can deny it all you like, but ignoring the truth does little to change it. This is us at our most harmonious with nature, our most productive—indeed our happiest, since for the first time in human history there are no laws, none at all. Every human being is free to do anything, so long as it is by the fruits of their labor. Only a very, very ill man would say this is a bad thing."

The man sat in the chair opposite me and took another sip. His tone became serious.

"I like you, Charles, I really do. Your heart is in the right place, even if you're too stupid to function. So I will do you the favor of being honest with you, of telling you something it takes most men a lifetime to learn. The only way to be an executive, and especially a CEO, is to be corrupt. The most corrupt always rise to the top the fastest. We are best suited to lead.

"By corrupt I do not mean, of course, debauched or ungodly, or publicly amoral. No, by definition corruption requires a positive image against which the corruption occurs. One must be able to portray oneself as infallible, as better than the rest, as always being true to one's word. One cannot, of course, run a business on those virtues; you'd be wiped out by a competitor that did not place such arbitrary limits on themselves. And you must corrupt yourself, Charles. You must convince yourself of your own infallibility in the face of any error of judgment. You must believe yourself superior to everyone."

"But I'm saying we don't have to live that way."

"It's the state of nature."

"We can evolve, we can make something better. We have language, we can work together in ways no animals can."

"And yet we remain animals. Life is difficult. I am sorry, but it is. And you're weak, so you'd rather not face it. Too weak to compete, you blame nature; you blame capitalism, you blame the system—everything but yourself. My god, how could a system be right if the great Charles Thatcher couldn't sit on his backside all day and make a million caps doing so?" The man paused. "It's sad, really."

"I worked hard."

"If that were true, you wouldn't be here."

He put the glass down and glared at me. "You're not even a man, when you think about it. A bit more like a dog, a creature that bites his owner's hand out of fear. Incapable of independent thought, only reaction. Greed is the most natural instinct in the world, and yet somehow you find new and never before seen ways of fighting against it. You are a dud, Charles, one of nature's failed experiments."

I looked at the floor. "My life is not a failure," I whispered.

"Oh, don't think about it too hard. You cannot help what you are. It's no more your fault that you can't understand these basic principles than it is my fault that you will suffer for it. Most people function only barely above your level. That's why they're most people. It's easier to believe that life isn't that way, that there is such a thing as freedom and that anyone can do anything if they put their mind to it. That's why executives need to spend so much time pretending success is possible for anyone. We have to *manufacture* hope, *manufacture* consent, and get people to *want* us to rule them. It's a difficult job, and frankly I'm not paid enough for it. But I find a way to get by, mostly because it's rewarding knowing I'm helping people."

My head hurt.

"People aren't that stupid," I whispered.

"Really? The single most basic economic principle in human history, known to every third grader in the world, is 'buy low, sell high.' We know it. It's an axiom. If it weren't, economics would fail to exist—there would be no system of making money; the universe would be in chaos.

"But what happens in an economic boom? Nobody sells stocks, they buy them. Why sell when maybe the price might go up even more? When the market crashes, as it always does, what happens? People sell, because they don't want to lose even more money. Buy low, sell high, a truism that nine in ten people can't follow. If they could, there would be no casinos, no exchanges, no gambling at all. And lord knows, I wouldn't make a dime on the markets. But I make money, a lot of it, because no matter how many times I tell people to buy low and sell high, nobody ever does. I can sit here and tell you everything I do to make money, exactly how to become rich and powerful, I can give away all the secrets to my success, and you wouldn't follow them—nobody would. Because they'd think they know better than I do, that the world will give them what they deserve in due time. And you say I'm arrogant? You say people aren't stupid? Thank God you're wrong, or I'd never have become an executive.

"And they do what you do. They blame the smart ones, those who can see the folly of man and survive despite of it. Nothing breeds hatred like success. That is Objectivism."

I'd noticed by now the absence of any clocks in the room, as if time itself did not exist within these four walls. The executive hadn't asked me a single question about Kate or the Republic. I didn't want to argue anymore, but I wouldn't abandon my beliefs, or my beloved Kate—real or imagined.

He's trying to shake my confidence. He's not asking me about her so I think he doesn't need to know, so I'll think she was Retention and then tell him everything.

"The pigs are walking," I mumbled.

"Oh my god, Charles, have you just figured that out? My friend, the pigs have been walking throughout all recorded history. What you have failed to realize is that there are three kinds of animals on our farm. There are the pigs, who are smart enough to take what is theirs; the horses, beasts on all fours who do what they're told; and at last the ducks, who point out that the pigs are walking but can't figure out just why it is that they wake up to find themselves with a bullet in the brain. You were too stupid to be a pig or a horse. So you sit there and shout from the top of your lungs 'the pigs are walking, the pigs are walking,' and you think you've seen something special, that *you're* special because you can see behind the curtain.

"But the truth is that everybody can see behind the curtain. Everybody knows that the pigs are walking. They accept that fact because they believe someday they will walk too.

"We've passed forty corporate budgets since I've been on the board. Do you know who pushes the hardest to lower the levies on HighCons? Epsilons, Zetas. Every poor man wants to cut levies on the wealthy because they all think that one day they will be that rich person, and if they help the HighCons, that karma will come around. Oh, they loathe executives, much like you do. But you always listened to your mentors. You didn't often heed their advice, but you listened, and you always tried to curry their favor.

"Yes, the pigs are walking. And everybody knows it. You're the only one who, for whatever reason, doesn't. You're a blind buffoon. You might as well run down the street naked shouting that the sky is blue.

"You accuse us of dogma?" he continued. "Of religious devotion to ideals in the face of overwhelming evidence? My god, your defects express themselves in so many ways, but this hypocrisy is truly astonishing. You are utterly incapable of reason, of self-reflection or critique, aren't you? It's a good thing, I suppose. We need defects like you to help remind people of how lucky they are."

The man had an answer for everything. He was wrong. I knew it, and would refuse to accept whatever he said, no matter what.

But that's the very deficit he's talking about, my stubborn refusal to accept even the most obvious facts.

It was a trick. This was what he did for a living, and he was far better at it than I was.

One of us is insane. I wonder if I can tell which?

"We are done for the day. I am sorry, but you are far more damaged than I anticipated. I'm afraid there is little I can do. The guards will take you back to your cell. Tomorrow morning they'll bring you back, and I'll tell you what's been decided."

21

As large as my cell was, with all the rooms and delicacies available to me, I felt the walls closing in. The suite was a living part of the system. It had become one of the most effective tools they had against me. It gave me every luxury I could hope for, more than I had ever imagined, but it would never give me answers. I wasn't sure of what was true anymore.

I had defied the executive, argued all of my points, but it was like trying to argue against gravity. I defended the republic, but my bulwarks were dismissed out of hand.

Maybe I've made a terrible mistake. Maybe I've been swimming upstream. Who am I to say that the system is wrong, and I'm right?

I had once believed in the absolute truth of the corporate system and its universal reflection of nature. I never liked it, but I accepted the truth of it. Then I met Kate, I learned about government, and I accepted that reality just as surely.

Maybe it was true, what they all said: reality doesn't exist outside of perception. Heck, maybe there was no such thing as reality.

I had been weak. I must have been. How else could I so easily slip from one belief to another? I understood this, but it still wouldn't change my fate. I was going to die at the hands of Retention. If I was lucky I might see the sky once more—just as they brought me out onto the stadium, onto the scaffolding and under the rope.

I had accepted that.

But I needed to know the truth. These realities could not both be right. To know the truth wouldn't save me, but I was long past caring about that.

If the crash came, if the world ended, the truth would be pretty clear. And there would be hope—a chance that maybe this horrific system could in fact be destroyed, by the only thing that could destroy it—itself. If the Republic survived then there would be those who would know that we could push back against our own nature. But if the crash was going to happen, I wouldn't live to see it. I was defeated, that wasn't in doubt. But if Kate had been real—if there really was a Republic—I would have seen something extraordinary.

I looked at my own reflection in the darkened television screen. Linus said that the person willing to risk the most won in poker. I no longer cared what happened to me. I could risk it all, and that would be my strength. I would make one last throw of the dice, and this time I would win.

22

Once again the guards left me in the foyer. Again I entered the master room, and again the executive emerged from the hallway in the back.

"I'm sorry, Charles," he said. "I'm afraid we still don't know what to do with you. You are beyond repair; I'm convinced of that. I let you down, and I am sorry. I was unable to fix you. Rest assured, I am among the best, and if I cannot do it... well, it cannot be done. If it's any consolation, there will be some profit in your death. Even factoring in the cost of trying to fix you and the damage you've done to the corp, the entirety of your life should net some small profit to Ackerman. That should please you."

"Why not just kill me?"

The executive looked disappointed. "Without profiting from it? My friend, how did you get this far before getting yourself in trouble?"

"When will you know what will happen to me?"

"I requested a public hanging. I think that would be the most profitable way to terminate you. You're a perfect candidate. But it's a tough negotiation; so many divisions have a say in the matter—Reclamation, Perception, Leisure, Entertainment, even Sales."

"Just end it. I'll volunteer for the rope. I don't want to be kept waiting."

"Goodness gracious, the delay is not out of any consideration for you. It's simply that there's a lot to deliberate. We have to be very careful how many people we hang publicly. Too many and the punishment becomes commonplace; we look callous and unforgiving, and people begin to wonder just why it is we have so many seditionists in the first place. But if we hang too few, then they might think we don't care about crime. And the condemned must look right—sufficiently broken that people believe they are truly sorry, but not so much as to evoke sympathy. We have to consider the whole aesthetic of it.

"Not to mention that we've hung a colleague from Perception two months in a row now. Three, and people may grouse that we're targeting them unfairly.

"And if Rendering had their way, there wouldn't be hangings at all. When you fall, your body pumps adrenaline into your bloodstream—makes your fat all stringy and harder to render properly; it just won't congeal right. They think that we should toss all of you straight into a vat of boiling water and lye. Oh, your death is a terribly complicated matter."

I nodded.

"You were difficult to place, Charles. I considered the gladiator ring for quite some time. I admit to thinking that perhaps might help you. After killing a few people you'd learn to appreciate the value of competition and be rehabilitated, if you survived. But you are broken even beyond that measure of repair. You'd just as likely put up no measurable resistance and let yourself get run through. That kind of foolishness doesn't make for rehabilitation, and certainly not for good television.

"Of course, there is no way to know what Reclamation will ultimately decide. I make my recommendation, but they can be unpredictable."

"Thank you for letting me know."

The executive looked sternly at me. He shook his head.

"I know a man. He loves to tell stories, little vignettes. I believe you know him, he's an Alpha."

"Linus Cabal," I said. "He's a high-ranked Beta, though."

The man laughed. "Linus? My friend, he hasn't been a Beta for quite some time. He's an Alpha—and a high one at that."

"That can't be. He's a Beta."

"He told you that he was a Beta. That you couldn't recognize him for what he was is not entirely surprising—he's really quite good at what he does, and you really are quite dim.

"In honor of Linus, I'll tell you my own little story. There was a HighCon barbershop—on the other side of the city. My father took me there twice a month. I met a child there, maybe five or six years old. The executives would come by every week and toy with him. They'd tell him that they would give him either a single cap or two quarters. Each time he would take the two quarters, and they would laugh and joke at how stupid he was.

"One day, and I must tell you this is probably the only time I've ever acted selflessly, I went up to him and said 'Don't you know that two quarters is half a cap?' He laughed. 'Of course I know.' I asked him why he kept taking the lesser amount. He said, 'Because the day I take the cap, they'll stop giving me quarters.' I made it my business to get to know that young man."

"Why are you telling me this?"

"Because I've known Linus a long time, Charles, and on his best day he's never gotten two quarters out of me."

"I don't under—"

"We're playing poker right now, you and I. You're pretending we're not, dancing around it, being conciliatory, and thinking I won't notice. But we've been playing since we met. You're the one who didn't realize it. So let's end this game. Ask me your question."

"I have no questions," I said.

"Ask."

"Was it Linus who turned me in?"

The executive sighed.

"That was not your question, but since you asked, I will tell you what I can. The truth is that Linus had high hopes for you, but he's been suspicious for quite some time."

"You call that efficiency? You send an Alpha to capture a Delta?"

"You overestimate your importance. He was not sent, he goes of his own accord. He's constantly looking for new talent, people the scouts miss. And where the scouts simply look for talent, he tries to foster it. Those who understand what he has to offer he often hires, takes them under his wing. The others he keeps an eye on, and if he sees anything suspicious, he turns them in for a nice profit."

"So he did turn me in."

"I didn't say that, nor do you care."

I laughed at the man who presumed to tell me what it was that I wanted to know.

"Despite my best efforts, you simply will not learn. I can read you like a book. I can read every twitch, every eye movement, and every curl of your lip. When you choose to be silent, when you think you are keeping everything from me, that is when I am learning the most."

"So when I am silent, I'm speaking to you?"

"Volumes."

"Then I won't say anything."

"It is too late. I know you in your entirety. Your problem is a lack of discipline. You have failed to devoid yourself of emotion. When you win you're happy, and when you lose you're sad. It's immature—you have the emotional control of… oh, probably a twelve-year-old. You have failed to understand that winning is temporary and only through the grace of God, and that losing it is just as temporary. There is never any need for happiness or sadness, to be arrogant or humble. A true Ackerman colleague has absolutely no emotion whatsoever. He is an employee, from the moment he wakes up to the moment he goes to bed—even in his dreams.

"Your failure to understand this has fostered this hope of yours for a better life. You hope that there is more than our Darwinist selves, that we can act in some way other than for our own pure, unadulterated self-interest, that somehow we are not human beings. One can either accept our nature or not. But you cannot change it, and your efforts to do so have done nothing but bring you misery and failure your entire life.

"Hope is a mental illness, a defect, very hard to cure. It is, by definition, the unwillingness to accept reality, the abandonment of rationality and reason for fantasy. You are psychotic, my friend, plain and simple

"Hope has brought you to this end, Charles, to this room. It's a common failure, though fortunately not often as severe as it is in your case. But hope is the flaw inherent to all low and MidCons. Everyone believes he is special, that he deserves what an executive has, that he can actually earn it. He believes that anyone can be an executive, that it's an easy job.

"We don't beat that hope out of them, because that belief drives them to work harder. But hope leads to expectations, and whatever joy you get when expectations are met is fleeting, and soon replaced with even greater expectations, until the inevitable outcome is reached; you have unrealistic expectations that can never be met. I have found few things that destroy a man faster than unrealistic expectations. Hope, therefore, truly is the death of the human spirit.

"To achieve something you must let go of your desire for it. You are too undisciplined to let go of your passions. That is why you are here, why you think you can win."

"Win what?"

"The answer to your question. Ask me what you want to know."

I looked at the executive, whose stare back was cold and callous.

"You cannot defeat me," he said. "You can get nothing from me that I do not choose to give you. You are already broken. You were born broken. You were born to come into this room and do anything I want. You are incapable of anything else. You simply don't comprehend it."

"I don't know what you're—"

The man opened his jacket pocket, reached inside and pulled out a revolver.

All at once I panicked. I had thought I was ready to die. Now that it was about to happen, I was terror struck.

His mood changed. He looked mean, vicious, and violent. The pillar of self-control, the master of the universe, had vanished, replaced with murderous hatred.

He slammed the pistol onto the table, threw open the poker set and slammed both cups down in front of me. He released his own cup, but held onto mine, the pistol resting between us.

"If you want to play, let's play."

I looked at the table.

"If you win, I will pay your debt to Ackerman myself and see your life spared," he said angrily. "They'll throw you out, but you'll live."

"If I lose?"

He glanced at the pistol.

"Five twos," he said.

The truth was that every game of poker that had ever mattered to me, the times I most believed that, with enough heart, desire, and will, I could grab a win, I was wrong. My hope failed me every time.

He knew I was no good at poker. And he placed a staggering bet. Five twos? The odds were five to one against him, maybe more. Yet he knew those odds and bet anyway—hadn't even looked at his own dice.

The dice could have been loaded, or nothing but two's on all sides. In that room he was a master of the universe, he could bend the very laws of probability to his will.

He had the five twos. I knew it. By luck or design, he had them. If I called or raised, I'd never leave the room alive.

I slumped back into the couch, head held in my hands.

He wasn't smug, didn't show any sign of pleasure at winning. He wouldn't even give me that much credit. He deftly slid the revolver back into his coat and scooped up the dice.

Not even an I-told-you-so.

He returned the shooters to their respective places and closed the lid. He ran his hands over the box ceremoniously. If the man derived pleasure from anything, it was from this box, the principal tool of his work.

"Why don't you just ask me your question?" the man said. "Is it so hard? Is your cowardice really that great?"

I was defeated, in every sense of the word. Calm washed over me. I had nothing to fear anymore. He would do what he wanted to me, when he wanted. Nothing I could do would have the slightest influence on my life from that point on.

"Was Kate in on it?" I asked.

He took a deep breath. "Congratulations. It cost you everything, Charles, but you finally reached the point where you could ask. Now, finally, at the end of things, you've become a man. Well done."

"Was she?"

There was a buzz at the door.

"I'm sorry, Charles. Our session ran longer than I thought it would. That would be Reclamation. You will be in their hands now. They will tell you your fate. Honestly, I do not know what it will be. But may you die well."

"Just tell me if she was in on it."

Two men came in through the door. He nodded toward me, and they grabbed me under each arm. I had no pride or self-respect left—it had all been bartered away.

"Please," I pleaded. "It costs you nothing to tell me. I just need to know."

"We're done here."

I knew at that moment that I would be sent to the gallows. I'd have a couple of weeks, maybe a month or two, but someday soon I would find myself there, on the first Monday of the month, walking up those worn, rickety steps. I'd be the one people talked about, one of those whose lives were extinguished publicly for money. In the canteens they would say things like, "Did you know how he betrayed the corporation?" and "He's a horrible little creature." But I could stand on that platform with dignity, if I knew the answer to a single question.

"Was she real?"

"I'm not going to tell you."

"Why not?"

"Because, Charles, you can't afford it."

Excerpt from The Executive Letters:

... I am not sure where you get this reverence for the proletariat, my friend, but I've heard it said that the best argument against democracy is ten minutes with the common man. Citizens love to talk about the power of the people, the abuses of power by fascist and totalitarian régimes like Adolf Hitler's. But they gloss over the fact that Hitler was democratically elected—elected, my friend, by your 'salt of the earth' common man.

Indeed, while they claim to know what they want—some measure of guarantee of free food, water and shelter—the truth is that they are completely ignorant of their own needs. Giving a man what he wants is, as often as not, a curse more than a blessing.

I want nothing more than to be generous, to give to people that which they need. I suffer terribly when someone dies from lack of food, water, or medical attention. But what you fail to realize is that generosity is the very antithesis of civilization. It makes people soft and lazy, increases their expectations and expends limited resources faster than nature can support (you seem to suggest that we just let people go around breathing air willy-nilly).

Human beings naturally reach a state of equilibrium. Give them half a gallon of water a day, they'll want a gallon. Give them a gallon; they'll swear they need two. Give them two, and they'll bemoan not having four. They can be equally content with half a gallon as with ten so long as you manage their perception—their sense of what they deserve—and their sense of hope—of that which they can reasonably obtain. The work of managing those expectations falls to executives. That, my dear friend, is a terrible burden, one lower contracts should consider themselves lucky they don't carry.

Value is earned. Therefore, by definition, anything given away cannot have value. Even food has value only because it is a limited resource.

I'd love to be generous. I hate hoarding resources. But as I said before, generosity is the enemy of the people, of civilization. It is the men who can do anything, the man who, like myself, takes money from the poor and bread from the hungry, we are the ones who save society, who save life, by being able to do that which lower contracts cannot. I do not heed their opinion of me or my work, their happiness or despair. They are nothing more than a number, the final line on a ledger sheet, and that is how they know I love them. Because it is for all mankind that I resist the temptation to be generous.

Generosity is selfishness. It is betraying your natural instinct to compete for a desire to play God, for the sense of self-satisfaction, that you have bestowed on a man more than he earned for himself. It is nothing less than sacrificing all of society for your own ego....